Enid Blyton®

THE FAMOUS FIVE
Treasury

HODDER CHILDREN'S BOOKS
First published in Great Britain in 2017 by Hodder and Stoughton

3 5 7 9 10 8 6 4 2

Illustrations by Laura Ellen Anderson
Additional illustrations by Atomic Squib

The books in The Famous Five series
were originally published by Hodder and Stoughton between 1942 and 1963.

Happy Christmas, Five! short story
originally published in *Princess Gift Book for Girls*, 1961
Well Done, Famous Five short story
originally published in *Australian Weeties Strip Book* series, 1956
Five Have a Puzzling Time short story
originally published in *Princess* magazine, 1960
Five and a Half-Term Adventure short story
originally published in *Enid Blyton's Magazine Annual 3*, 1956
A Lazy Afternoon short story
originally published in *Enid Blyton's Magazine Annual 1*, 1954

A CIP catalogue record for this book is available from the British Library.

ISBN 978 1 444 93938 5

Printed and bound in China by RR Donnelley Asia Printing Solutions Limited

The paper and board used in this book are made from wood from responsible sources.

Hodder Children's Books
An imprint of
Hachette Children's Group
Part of Hodder and Stoughton
Carmelite House
50 Victoria Embankment
London EC4Y 0DZ

An Hachette UK Company
www.hachette.co.uk
www.hachettechildrens.co.uk

Enid Blyton®

THE FAMOUS FIVE Treasury

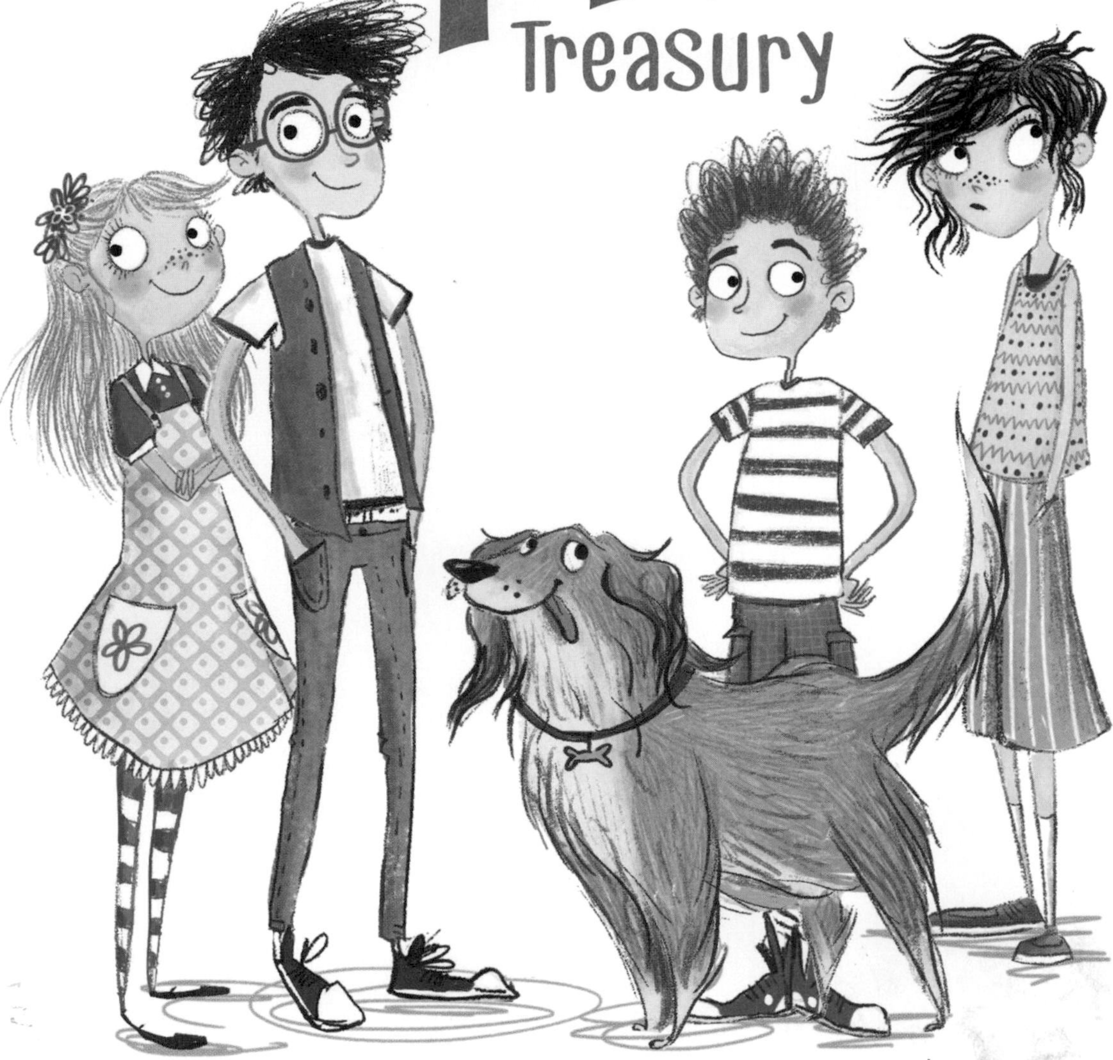

With Illustrations by Laura Ellen Anderson

CONTENTS

CHRISTMAS with THE FAMOUS FIVE

HAPPY CHRISTMAS, FIVE!

Christmas Eve at Kirrin Cottage – and the Five were all there together! They were up in the boys' bedroom, wrapping Christmas presents in bright paper. Timmy was very excited, and nosed about the room, his long tail wagging in delight.

'Don't keep slapping my legs with your tail, Tim,' said Anne. 'Look out, George, he's getting tangled up with your ball of string!'

'Don't look round, Anne, I'm wrapping up your present,' said Dick. 'There'll be a lot to give out this Christmas, with all of us here – and everyone giving everyone else something!'

'I've a B-O-N-E for Timmy,' said Anne, 'but it's downstairs in the larder. I was afraid he'd sniff it out up here.'

'Woof,' said Timmy, slapping his tail against Anne's legs again.

'He knows perfectly well that B-O-N-E spells bone,' said Julian. 'Now you've made him sniff all about my parcels! Timmy – go downstairs, please!'

'Oh no – he does so love Christmas time, and helping us to wrap up parcels,' said George. 'Sit, Timmy. SIT, I say. That's the third time you've knocked down my pile of presents.'

Downstairs, her father and mother were wrapping up parcels, too. They seemed to have as many as the four cousins upstairs! Mrs Kirrin looked at the pile of packages on the table.

'Far too many to go on the tree!' she said. 'We'd better put all our parcels and the children's too into a sack, Quentin. We can stand the sack at the bottom of the tree, and you can be Father Christmas and hand them out tomorrow morning.'

'I am NOT going to be Father Christmas,' said Mr Kirrin. 'All this nonsense at Christmas time! Bits of paper everywhere – parcels to undo – Timmy barking his head off. Listen to him now! I'll go mad! He's to go to his kennel.'

'No, no, Quentin – don't upset George on Christmas Eve,' said Mrs Kirrin. 'Look – you go and sit down quietly in your study and read the paper. I'll finish the parcels. But you MUST be good and hand them out to the children tomorrow morning – yes, and hand Timmy's to him too.'

Supper-time came all too soon that night. When the bell rang to tell the Five that the meal was ready, they groaned.

'Have to finish afterwards,' said Dick, looking round at the mess of parcels, paper, string, ribbon and labels. 'Supper, Timmy, supper!'

Timmy shot downstairs at top speed, bumping heavily into Mr Kirrin, who was just coming out of his study. Timmy gave him a quick lick of apology, and ran into the dining-room, putting his front feet on the table to see what was there.

'Down, Timmy – what manners!' said Julian. 'Hello, Uncle Quentin – done up all your parcels yet?'

His uncle grunted. Aunt Fanny laughed. 'He's going to be Father Christmas tomorrow morning and hand out all the presents,' she said. 'Don't scowl like that, Quentin dear – you look just like George when I tell her to fetch something!'

'I do NOT scowl,' said George, scowling immediately, of course. Everyone roared at her, and she had to smile.

'Christmas Day tomorrow,' said Anne happily. 'Aunt Fanny, it's lovely of you to have us all here for Christmas. We'll never finish opening our parcels tomorrow morning! I've got at least one for everybody, and so has everyone else.'

'A nice little bit of arithmetic,' said Julian. 'That means we've about forty or more presents to undo – counting in those for Joanna and Timmy.'

'What a waste of time!' That remark came from Uncle Quentin, of course!

'It's a good thing you're not as horrible as you pretend to be, Dad,' said George, and grinned at him. 'You always look so fierce – and yet I bet you've been round the shops buying all kinds of things. Hasn't he, Mum? I bet he's bought Timmy something, too.'

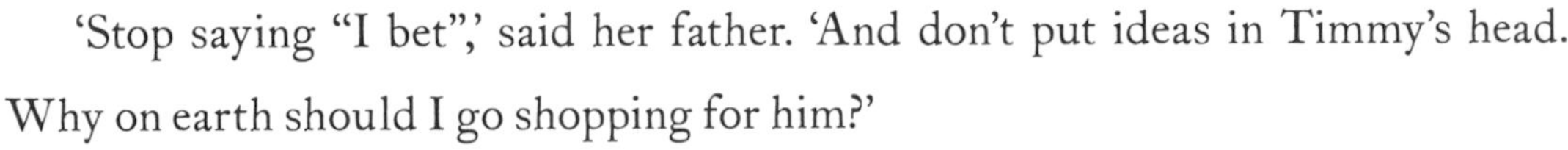

'Stop saying "I bet",' said her father. 'And don't put ideas in Timmy's head. Why on earth should I go shopping for him?'

'Woof!' said Timmy, from under the table, delighted to hear his name. He wagged his tail violently and Mr Kirrin leapt to his feet with a yell.

'Take that dog out! Slapping me with his tail like that! Why can't he have a short tail? I'll . . .'

'Sit down, Quentin,' said his wife. 'Timmy, come out. Sit over there. Now – let's change the subject!'

The four cousins looked at one another and grinned. It was lovely to be at Kirrin Cottage again, with dear kind Aunt Fanny, and quick-tempered Uncle Quentin. He was now beaming round at them, offering them a second helping.

'No thanks,' said Dick. 'I'm saving up for the pudding. I spotted it in the larder – scrumptious!'

After supper they finished their parcels, and brought them all down to the sitting-room.

The tree was there, looking very cheerful, although the candles on it were not yet lit. It was hung with tinsel and little sparkling ornaments, and had at the top the fairy doll that had been on every Christmas tree since George was little.

The parcels were put into a big sack, and this was set at the foot of the tree, ready for the morning. Timmy immediately went to sniff at it, from top to bottom.

'He can smell his Christmas bone,' said Anne. 'Timmy, come away. I won't have you guessing my present!'

Later they played games, and Timmy joined in. He was so excited that he began to bark, and Uncle Quentin stormed out of his study at once, and appeared in the sitting-room.

'George! I've told you before I won't have Timmy barking in the house. Yes, I know it's Christmas Eve, but I can't STAND that barking. Why must he have such a loud one? It's enough to deafen me. I'll turn him out. He can go to his kennel!'

'Oh no, Dad – not on Christmas Eve!' said George, horrified. 'Timmy, go and lie down – and BE QUIET!'

'He's to go out to his kennel,' said her father. 'That's my last word. Out, Timmy, OUT!'

So out poor Timmy had to go, his tail well down. He felt puzzled. The children had been shouting, hadn't they? It was their way of barking. Well, why couldn't he shout in his own way, which was barking?

George was cross, and Anne was almost in tears. Poor Timmy – to be sent out to his kennel on Christmas Eve! She went to comfort George, and was surprised to see that she wasn't looking upset.

'Don't worry, Anne – I'll fetch him in when we go to bed and he can sleep in our room as usual,' she said.

'You can't do that!' said Anne. 'Uncle Quentin would be furious if he discovered him there.'

'He won't,' said George. 'It's no good, Anne – I'm going to have Timmy with me tonight, although I KNOW I shouldn't. I couldn't bear not to. I'll own up to Dad tomorrow.'

So, when the household was safely in bed, George crept downstairs to fetch Timmy from his kennel. He whined softly in joy and wagged his big tail.

'Be quiet now,' whispered George, and she took him upstairs – completely forgetting to lock the kitchen door!

Timmy settled down on the rug beside her bed, very happy, and soon Anne and George were fast asleep in their beds, while the two boys slept soundly in their room nearby.

All four were awakened by a terrific bout of barking from Timmy! He stood at the bedroom door, scraping at it, trying to open it, barking at the top of his voice! George leapt out of bed in alarm.

'What is it, Timmy? What is it? Stop barking – Dad'll hear you and know

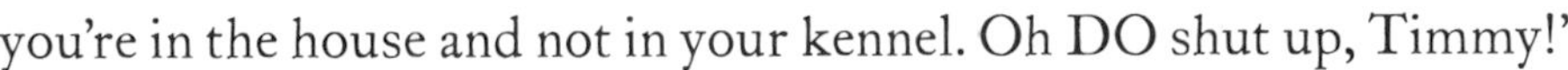

you're in the house and not in your kennel. Oh DO shut up, Timmy!'

But by this time everyone was wide awake, and soon the whole household was out on the landing, alarmed. George's father was very angry when he saw that Timmy was in the house after all.

'Why isn't he in his kennel? What's the matter with him? How DARE you disobey me, George?'

'Take him out to his kennel at once, George,' said her mother, very cross too. 'He's over-excited tonight – it was all that fun and games you had. Take him out at once.'

'But, Mum – he doesn't usually bark. Perhaps there was a burglar in the house,' said poor George.

'Nonsense!' said her father, angrily. 'No burglar would come on Christmas Eve. Take the dog out to his kennel – and don't let me hear another sound tonight!'

'Go on, George, now,' said her mother. 'Do as you're told and don't spoil Christmas.' Timmy was very sad to be put into his kennel again. He whined dismally, and George almost made up her mind to stay outside with him.

But his kennel wasn't big enough to take both of them, so she gave him a hug and went indoors with Anne, scowling in the darkness.

This time she remembered to lock the door behind her! Soon everyone was in bed again, and sound asleep.

Anne awoke a little while later and sat up in bed. She had heard something – some noise downstairs. She sat and listened. Was there someone in the sitting-room? Then she heard a click. 'Like a door being shut,' she thought, and wondered if she should wake George.

No – surely Timmy would bark loudly if he heard anything suspicious – he was only just outside, in his kennel. Perhaps he *had* heard something when he had barked before.

'Well, anyway, I'm not going downstairs by myself in the dark,' thought Anne. 'And I really daren't wake Uncle or Aunt. I must leave Timmy to deal with whatever it is. He can always bark or howl if someone is about!'

Timmy had heard something, and he was sitting in his kennel, ears pricked up, a little growl grumbling in his throat. He really didn't dare to bark this time. He had heard something before, when he had barked in George's bedroom, and awakened the whole household – and yet there had been nobody downstairs then that he could see or smell!

But somebody was in the house – someone who had crept in at the kitchen door, when George had left it unlocked!

That Somebody had hidden in the coal cellar, door fast shut, when Timmy had barked and alarmed the household! Now the Somebody was about again, switching on a small torch, making the little noises that had awakened Anne.

It was Tom, the bad boy of the village! He had been out to a rowdy party, and had passed Kirrin Cottage on his way home. He had tiptoed to the front door, and gone to the garden door and tried both handles – no, they were locked! Then he had slipped round to the kitchen door, and to his surprise and delight had found it opened when he turned the handle.

He had crept inside and was just looking round when Timmy had begun to bark upstairs – and quick as a rabbit Tom had slipped into the coal cellar, and shivered there while the household came out on to the landing, angry with Timmy, who was then put into his kennel.

When all was quiet, and the dog safely in his kennel, the boy looked quietly round to see what he could take. He thought he heard a noise, and stopped in alarm. No, it was only the coals dropping in the grate. He felt scared, and swung his torch round and about to see what he could easily take away with him.

He saw the sack lying by the Christmas tree – how it bulged with the parcels inside it! Tom grinned in delight. 'Must be full of wonderful presents!' he thought. 'All nicely bundled up in a sack, too – couldn't be easier for me to carry!'

He lifted it, put it over his shoulder, and tiptoed out of the kitchen door,

shutting it with a little click – the click that Anne had heard from upstairs!

Timmy knew there was someone about, of course – but now he didn't dare to bark. He had been put into his kennel as a punishment for barking – if he barked again and woke Mr Kirrin, goodness knows what would happen to him!

So he kept completely silent, and slipped out of his kennel, and down the garden path after the boy with the sack. He followed him all the way to the village, unseen and unheard. How he longed to growl, how he longed to fly at this nasty little robber-boy and nip him sharply in the leg!

He saw the boy go through a gate and walk to a shed nearby. He went in, and came out again – but this time without the sack! Then he let himself into the house nearby, shut the door, and disappeared.

Timmy sat down to think. After a minute he went to the shed and slipped through the half-broken wooden door.

He smelt the sack at once. That bulging sack belonged to George! Very well – it must at once be taken back to Kirrin Cottage before the boy took out all the presents in it. Timmy sniffed at the parcels inside. His own parcel was there – the one with the bone that Anne had wrapped up for him.

Timmy growled. So that boy had DARED to carry away his bone! Timmy decided to take the whole sack back to Kirrin Cottage.

But it was far too heavy for him to drag out of the shed! What was he to do?

He worked his head into the open sack neck again and pulled out a parcel – then another and another! Good – he would take them one by one to his kennel and hide them there for Christmas morning!

And that is exactly what dear, patient Timmy did! He took all those parcels one by one to his kennel, trotting back and forth so many times that he began to feel he was walking in a dream!

It was lucky that Kirrin Cottage wasn't far from the boy's home, or Timmy would have been trotting to and fro all night!

At last the sack was empty, and the last parcel safely tucked into the back of his big kennel.

There was hardly room for Timmy to sit in it! Tired out but very happy, he put down his head on his paws, and fell sound asleep.

He was awakened next morning by a great hubbub in Kirrin Cottage!

'Aunt Fanny! Uncle Quentin! The sack of presents is gone – and the kitchen door's wide open! Someone's stolen all our presents in the night.'

'That's why Timmy barked! He knew there was something going on! Oh, our beautiful presents! What a MEAN trick!'

'But why didn't Tim catch the thief when he slipped out of the kitchen door with the sack? Poor Tim – he must have been too scared to do anything, after being scolded for barking before, and made to go to his kennel!'

'Christmas is spoilt!' said Anne, with tears in her eyes. 'No presents at all – no surprises – no fun!'

'Woof!' said Timmy, coming out of his kennel, as the four children came up the path. 'Woof!'

'Who took our lovely presents, Timmy – and where do you think they are now?' said George, sorrowfully. 'Didn't you dare to bark?'

'Woof,' said Timmy, in an apologetic voice, and went into his kennel.

He backed out with something in his mouth – a parcel! He went in and fetched another – and another – and another!

He laid them all down in front of the astounded children, wagging his tail.

'TIMMY! Where did you get them? Where's the sack? Did you chase the thief, and take the parcels one by one out of the sack – and bring them home?' asked George, in wonder.

'Woof,' said Timmy, agreeing, and wagged his tail vigorously. He pawed at one of the parcels, and Anne gave a delighted laugh.

'That's my present to you!' she said. 'You knew it was for you, Tim – you smelt

the bone inside.'

'Darling, darling Tim, how clever you are! You stored all our presents safely in your kennel, so that we'd have them on Christmas morning after all! I'll undo your parcel and you'll have my present first of all!'

'WOOF, WOOF, WOOF!' barked Timmy, in delight, and not even Uncle Quentin frowned at the tremendous noise.

'Good old Timmy! Open your parcel and then go indoors and gnaw your bone, while you watch the others open theirs.'

Happy Christmas to all the Five – and especially to you, Timmy-dog, especially to you!

CHRISTMAS AT KIRRIN COTTAGE

Much to Dick's disgust, the children have a tutor called Mr Roland in the Christmas holidays.

For the next day or two the four children did not really have much time to think about the Secret Way, because Christmas was coming near, and there was a good deal to do.

There were Christmas cards to draw and paint for their mothers and fathers and friends. There was the house to decorate. They went out with Mr Roland to find sprays of holly, and came home laden.

'You look like a Christmas card yourselves,' said Aunt Fanny, as they walked up the garden path, carrying the red-berried holly over their shoulders. Mr Roland had found a group of trees with tufts of mistletoe growing from the top branches, and they had brought some of that too. Its berries shone like pale green pearls.

'Mr Roland had to climb the tree to get this,' said Anne. 'He's a good climber – as good as a monkey.'

Everyone laughed except George. She never laughed at anything to do with the tutor. They all dumped their loads down in the porch, and went to wash. They were to decorate the house that evening.

'Is Uncle going to let his study be decorated too?' asked Anne. There were all kinds of strange instruments and glass tubes in the study now, and the children looked at them with wonder whenever they ventured into the study, which was very seldom.

'No, my study is certainly not to be messed about,' said Uncle Quentin, at once. 'I wouldn't hear of it.'

'Uncle, why do you have all these funny things in your study?' asked Anne, looking round with wide eyes.

Uncle Quentin laughed. 'I'm looking for a secret formula!' he said.

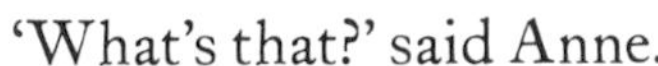

'What's that?' said Anne.

'You wouldn't understand,' said her uncle. 'All these "funny things" as you call them, help me in my experiments, and I put down in my book what they tell me – and from all I learn I work out a secret formula, which will be of great use when it is finished.'

'You want to know a secret formula, and we want to know a secret way,' said Anne, quite forgetting that she was not supposed to talk about this.

Julian was standing by the door. He frowned at Anne. Luckily Uncle Quentin was not paying any more attention to the little girl's chatter. Julian pulled her out of the room.

'Anne, the only way to stop you giving away secrets is to sew up your mouth, like Brer Rabbit wanted to do to Mister Dog!' he said.

Joanna the cook was busy baking Christmas cakes. An enormous turkey had been sent over from Kirrin Farm, and was hanging up in the larder. Timothy thought it smelt glorious, and Joanna was always shooing him out of the kitchen.

There were boxes of crackers on the shelf in the sitting-room, and mysterious parcels everywhere. It was very, very Christmassy! The children were happy and excited.

Mr Roland went out and dug up a little spruce fir tree. 'We must have a Christmas tree,' he said. 'Have you any tree-ornaments, children?'

'No,' said Julian, seeing George shake her head.

'I'll go into the town this afternoon and get some for you,' promised the tutor. 'It will be fun dressing the tree. We'll put it in the hall, and light candles on it on Christmas Day after tea. Who's coming with me to get the candles and the ornaments?'

'I am!' cried three children. But the fourth said nothing. That was George. Not even to buy tree-ornaments would the obstinate little girl go with Mr Roland.

Now the tree stood in the hall, with coloured candles in holders clipped to the branches, and bright shining ornaments hanging from top to bottom. Silver strands of frosted string hung down from the branches like icicles, and Anne had put bits of white cotton wool here and there to look like snow. It really was a lovely sight to see.

'Beautiful!' said Uncle Quentin, as he passed through the hall, and saw Mr Roland hanging the last ornaments on the tree. 'I say – look at the fairy doll on the top! Who's that for? A good girl?'

Anne secretly hoped that Mr Roland would give her the doll. She was sure it wasn't for George – and anyway, George wouldn't accept it. It was such a pretty doll, with its gauzy frock and silvery wings.

Julian, Dick and Anne had quite accepted the tutor now as teacher and friend. In fact, everyone had, their uncle and aunt too, and even Joanna the cook. George, of course, was the only exception, and she and Timothy kept away from Mr Roland, each looking as sulky as the other whenever the tutor was in the room.

'You know, I never knew a dog could look so sulky!' said Julian, watching Timothy. 'Really, he scowls almost like George.'

'And I always feel as if George puts her tail down like Tim, when Mr Roland is in the room,' giggled Anne.

'Laugh all you like,' said George, in a low tone. 'I think you're beastly to me. I know I'm right about Mr Roland. I've got a feeling about him. And so has Tim.'

'You're silly, George,' said Dick. 'You haven't really got a feeling – it's only that Mr Roland will keep calling you Georgina and putting you in your place, and that he doesn't like Tim. I dare say he can't help disliking dogs. After all, there was once a famous man called Lord Roberts who couldn't bear cats.'

'Oh well, cats are different,' said George. 'If a person doesn't like dogs, especially a dog like our Timothy, then there really must be something wrong with him.'

'It's no use arguing with George,' said Julian. 'Once she's made up her mind about something, she won't budge!'

George went out of the room in a huff. The others thought she was behaving rather stupidly.

'I'm surprised really,' said Anne. 'She was so jolly last term at school. Now she's gone all strange, rather like she was when we first knew her last summer.'

'I do think Mr Roland has been decent digging up the Christmas tree and everything,' said Dick. 'I still don't like him awfully much sometimes, but I think he's a sport. What about asking him if he can read that old linen rag for us – I don't think I'd mind him sharing our secret, really.'

'I would love him to share it,' said Anne, who was busy doing a marvellous Christmas card for the tutor. 'He's most awfully clever. I'm sure he could tell us what the Secret Way is. Do let's ask him.'

'All right,' said Julian. 'I'll show him the piece of linen. It's Christmas Eve tonight. He will be with us in the sitting-room, because Aunt Fanny is going into the study with Uncle Quentin to wrap up presents for all of us!'

So, that evening, before Mr Roland came in to sit with them, Julian took out the little roll of linen and stroked it out flat on the table. George looked at it in surprise.

'Mr Roland will be here in a minute,' she said. 'You'd better put it away quickly.'

'We're going to ask him if he can tell us what the old Latin words mean,' said Julian.

'You're not!' cried George, in dismay. 'Ask him to share our secret! How ever can you?'

'Well, we want to know what the secret is, don't we?' said Julian. 'We don't need to tell him where we got this or anything about it except that we want to know what the markings mean. We're not exactly sharing the secret with him – only asking him to use his brains to help us.'

'Well, I never thought you'd ask him,' said George. 'And he'll want to know simply everything about it, you just see if he won't! He's terribly snoopy.'

'Whatever do you mean?' said Julian, in surprise. 'I don't think he's a bit snoopy.'

'I saw him yesterday snooping round the study when no one was there,' said George. 'He didn't see me outside the window with Tim. He was having a real poke round.'

'You know how interested he is in your father's work,' said Julian. 'Why shouldn't he look at it? Your father likes him too. You're just seeing what horrid things you can find to say about Mr Roland.'

'Oh shut up, you two,' said Dick. 'It's Christmas Eve. Don't let's argue or quarrel or say beastly things.'

Just at that moment the tutor came into the room. 'All as busy as bees?' he said, his mouth smiling beneath its moustache. 'Too busy to have a game of cards, I suppose?'

'Mr Roland, sir,' began Julian, 'could you help us with something? We've got an old bit of linen here with odd markings on it. The words seem to be in some sort of Latin and we can't make them out.'

George gave an angry exclamation as she saw Julian push the piece of linen over towards the tutor. She went out of the room and shut the door with a bang. Tim was with her.

'Our sweet-tempered Georgina doesn't seem to be very friendly tonight,' remarked Mr Roland, pulling the bit of linen towards him. 'Where in the world did you get this? What an odd thing!'

Nobody answered. Mr Roland studied the roll of linen, and then gave an exclamation. 'Ah – I see why you wanted to know the meaning of those Latin words the other day – the ones that meant "hidden path", you remember. They are at the top of this linen roll.'

'Yes,' said Dick. All the children leaned over towards Mr Roland, hoping he would be able to unravel a little of the mystery for them.

'We just want to know the meaning of the words, sir,' said Julian.

'This is really very interesting,' said the tutor, puzzling over the linen.

'Apparently there are directions here for finding the opening or entrance of a secret path or road.'

'That's what we thought!' cried Julian, excitedly. 'That's exactly what we thought. Oh, sir, do read the directions and see what you make of them.'

'Well, these eight squares are meant to represent wooden boards or panels, I think,' said the tutor, pointing to the eight rough squares drawn on the linen. 'Wait a minute – I can hardly read some of the words. This is most fascinating. Solum lapideum – paries ligneus – and what's this? – cellula – yes, cellula!'

The children hung on his words. 'Wooden panels!' That must mean panels somewhere at Kirrin Farmhouse.

Mr Roland frowned down at the old printed words.

Then he sent Anne to borrow a magnifying glass from her uncle. She came back with it, and the four of them looked through the glass, seeing the words three times as clearly now.

'Well,' said the tutor at last, 'as far as I can make out the directions mean this: a room facing east; eight wooden panels, with an opening somewhere to be found in that marked one; a stone floor – yes, I think that's right, a stone floor, and a cupboard. It all sounds most extraordinary and very thrilling. Where did you get this from?'

'We just found it,' said Julian, after a pause. 'Oh, Mr Roland, thanks awfully. We could never have made it out by ourselves. I suppose the entrance to the Secret Way is in a room facing east then.'

'It looks like it,' said Mr Roland, poring over the linen roll again. 'Where did you say you found this?'

'We didn't say,' said Dick. 'It's a secret really, you see.'

'I think you might tell me,' said the tutor, looking at Dick with his brilliant blue eyes. 'I can be trusted with secrets. You've no idea how many strange secrets I know.'

'Well,' said Julian, 'I don't really see why you shouldn't know where we found this, Mr Roland. We found it at Kirrin Farmhouse, in an old tobacco pouch. I suppose the Secret Way begins somewhere there! I wonder where and wherever can it lead to?'

'You found it at Kirrin Farmhouse!' exclaimed Mr Roland. 'Well, well – I must say that seems to be an interesting old place. I shall have to go over there one day.'

Julian rolled up the piece of linen and put it into his pocket. 'Well, thank you, sir,' he said. 'You've solved a bit of the mystery for us but set another puzzle! We must look for the entrance of the Secret Way after Christmas, when we can walk over to Kirrin Farmhouse.'

'I'll come with you,' said Mr Roland. 'I may be able to help a little. That is – if you don't mind me having a little share in this exciting secret.'

'Well – you've been such a help in telling us what the words mean,' said Julian, 'we'd like you to come if you want to, sir.'

'Yes, we would,' said Anne.

'We'll go and look for the Secret Way, then,' said Mr Roland. 'What fun we shall have, tapping round the panels, waiting for a mysterious dark entrance to appear!'

'I don't suppose George will go,' Dick murmured to Julian. 'You shouldn't have said Mr Roland could go with us, Ju. That means that old George will have to be left out of it. You know how she hates that.'

'I know,' said Julian, feeling uncomfortable. 'Don't let's worry about that now though. George may feel different after Christmas. She can't keep up this kind of behaviour for ever!'

* * *

It was great fun on Christmas morning. The children awoke early and tumbled out of bed to look at the presents that were stacked on chairs nearby.

Squeals and yells of delight came from everyone.

'Oh! a railway station! Just what I wanted! Who gave me this marvellous station?'

'A new doll – with eyes that shut! I shall call her Betsy-May. She looks just like a Betsy-May!'

'I say – what a whopping great book – all about aeroplanes. From Aunt Fanny! How decent of her!'

'Timothy! Look what Julian has given you – a collar with big brass studs all round – you will be grand. Go and lick him to say thank you!'

'Who's this from? I say, who gave me this? Where's the label? Oh – from Mr Roland. How decent of him! Look, Julian, a pocket-knife with three blades!'

So the cries and exclamations went on, and the four excited children and the equally excited dog spent a glorious hour before a late Christmas breakfast, opening all kinds and shapes of parcels. The bedrooms were in a fine mess when the children had finished!

'Who gave you that book about dogs, George?' asked Julian, seeing rather a nice dog book lying on George's pile.

'Mr Roland,' said George, rather shortly. Julian wondered if George was going to accept it. He rather thought she wouldn't. But the little girl, defiant and obstinate as she was, had made up her mind not to spoil Christmas Day by being 'difficult'. So, when the others thanked the tutor for their things she too added her thanks, though in rather a stiff little voice.

George had not given the tutor anything, but the others had, and Mr Roland thanked them all very heartily, appearing to be very pleased indeed. He told Anne that her Christmas card was the nicest he had ever had, and she beamed at him with joy.

'Well, I must say it's nice to be here for Christmas!' said Mr Roland, when he and the others were sitting round a loaded Christmas table, at the midday dinner.

'Shall I carve for you, Mr Kirrin? I'm good at that!'

Uncle Quentin handed him the carving knife and fork gladly. 'It's nice to have you here,' he said warmly. 'I must say you've settled in well – I'm sure we all feel as if we've known you for ages!'

It really was a jolly Christmas Day. There were no lessons, of course, and there were to be none the next day either. The children gave themselves up to the enjoyment of eating a great deal, sucking sweets, and looking forward to the lighting of the Christmas tree.

It looked beautiful when the candles were lighted. They twinkled in the darkness of the hall, and the bright ornaments shone and glowed. Tim sat and looked at it, quite entranced.

'He likes it as much as we do,' said George. And indeed Tim had enjoyed the day just as much as any of them.

They were all tired out when they went to bed.

'I shan't be long before I'm asleep,' yawned Anne. 'Oh, George – it's been fun, hasn't it? I did like the Christmas tree.'

'Yes, it's been lovely,' said George, jumping into bed. 'Here comes Mother to say good night. Basket, Tim, basket!'

Tim leapt into his basket by the window. He was always there when George's mother came into say good night to the girls but as soon as she had gone downstairs, the dog took a flying leap and landed on George's bed. There he slept, his head curled round her feet.

'Don't you think Tim ought to sleep downstairs tonight?' said George's mother. 'Joanna says he ate such an enormous meal in the kitchen that she is sure he will be sick.'

'Oh no, Mother!' said George, at once. 'Make Tim sleep downstairs on Christmas night? Whatever would he think?'

'Oh, very well,' said her mother, with a laugh. 'I might have known it was useless to suggest it. Now to sleep quickly, Anne and George – it's late and you are all tired.'

She went into the boys' room and said good night to them too. They were almost asleep.

Two hours later everyone else was in bed. The house was still and dark. George and Anne slept peacefully in their small beds. Timothy slept too, lying heavily on George's feet.

Suddenly George awoke with a jump. Tim was growling softly! He had raised his big shaggy head and George knew that he was listening.

'What is it, Tim?' she whispered. Anne did not wake. Tim went on growling softly. George sat up and put her hand on his collar to stop him. She knew that if he awoke her father, he would be cross.

Timothy stopped growling now that he had roused George. The girl sat and wondered what to do. It wasn't any good waking Anne. The little girl would be frightened. Why was Tim growling? He never did that at night!

'Perhaps I'd better go and see if everything is all right,' thought George. She was quite fearless, and the thought of creeping through the still, dark house did not disturb her at all. Besides she had Tim! Who could be afraid with Tim beside them!

She slipped on her dressing-gown. 'Perhaps a log has fallen out of one of the fireplaces and a rug is burning,' she thought, sniffing as she went down the stairs. 'It would be just like Tim to smell it and warn us!'

With her hand on Tim's head to warn him to be quite quiet, George crept softly through the hall to the sitting-room. The fire was quite all right there – just a red glow. In the kitchen all was peace too. Tim's feet made a noise there, as his claws rattled against the linoleum.

A slight sound came from the other side of the house.

Tim growled quite loudly, and the hairs on the back of his neck rose up. George stood still. Could it possibly be burglars?

Suddenly Timothy shook himself free from her fingers and leapt across the hall, down a passage, and into the study beyond! There was the sound of an exclamation, and a noise as if someone was falling over.

'It is a burglar!' said George, and she ran to the study. She saw a torch shining on the floor, dropped by someone who was even now struggling with Tim.

George switched on the light, and then looked with the greatest astonishment into the study. Mr Roland was there in his dressing-gown, rolling on the floor, trying to get away from Timothy, who, although not biting him, was holding him firmly by his dressing-gown.

'Oh – it's you, George! Call your beastly dog off!' said Mr Roland, in a low and angry voice. 'Do you want to rouse all the household?'

'Why are you creeping about with a torch?' demanded George.

'I heard a noise down here, and came to see what it was,' said Mr Roland, sitting up and trying to fend off the angry dog. 'For goodness sake, call your beast off.'

'Why didn't you put on the light?' asked George, not attempting to take Tim away. She was very much enjoying the sight of an angry and frightened Mr Roland.

'I couldn't find it,' said the tutor. 'It's on the wrong side of the door, as you see.'

This was true. The switch was an awkward one to find if you didn't know it. Mr Roland tried to push Tim away again, and the dog suddenly barked.

'Well – he'll wake everyone!' said the tutor, angrily. 'I didn't want to rouse the house. I thought I could find out for myself if there was anyone about – a burglar perhaps. Here comes your father!'

George's father appeared, carrying a large poker.

He stood still in astonishment when he saw Mr Roland on the ground and Timothy standing over him.

'What's all this?' he exclaimed. Mr Roland tried to get up, but Tim would not let him. George's father called to him sternly.

'Tim! Come here, sir!'

Timothy glanced at George to see if his mistress agreed with her father's command. She said nothing. So Timothy took no notice of the order and merely made a snap at Mr Roland's ankles.

'That dog's mad!' said Mr Roland, from the floor. 'He's already bitten me once before, and now he's trying to do it again!'

'Tim! Will you come here, sir!' shouted George's father. 'George, that dog is really disobedient. Call him off at once.'

'Come here, Tim!' said George, in a low voice. The dog at once came to her, standing by her side with the hairs on his neck still rising up stiffly. He growled softly as if to say, 'Be careful, Mr Roland, be careful!'

The tutor got up. He was very angry indeed. He spoke to George's father.

'I heard some sort of noise and came down with my torch to see what it was,' he said. 'I thought it came from your study, and knowing you kept your valuable books and instruments here, I wondered if some thief was about. I had just got down, and into the room, when that dog appeared from somewhere and got me down on the ground! George came along too, and would not call him off.'

'I can't understand your behaviour, George; I really can't,' said her father, angrily. 'I hope you are not going to behave stupidly, as you used to behave before your cousins came last summer. And what is this I hear about Tim biting Mr Roland before?'

'George had him under the table during lessons,' said Mr Roland. 'I didn't know that, and when I stretched out my legs, they touched Tim, and he bit me. I didn't tell you before, sir, because I didn't want to trouble you. Both George and the dog have tried to annoy me ever since I have been here.'

'Well, Tim must go outside and live in the kennel,' said George's father. 'I won't have him in the house. It will be a punishment for him, and a punishment for you too, George. I will not have this kind of behaviour. Mr Roland has been extremely kind to you all.'

'I won't let Tim live outside,' said George furiously. 'It's such cold weather, and it would simply break his heart.'

'Well, his heart must be broken then,' said her father. 'It will depend entirely on your behaviour from now on whether Tim is allowed in the house at all these holidays. I shall ask Mr Roland each day how you have behaved. If you have a bad report, then Tim stays outside. Now you know! Go back to bed but first apologise to Mr Roland!'

'I won't!' said George, and choked by feelings of anger and dismay, she tore out of the room and up the stairs. The two men stared after her.

'Let her be,' said Mr Roland. 'She's a very difficult child – and has made up her mind not to like me, that's quite plain. But I shall be very glad to know that that dog isn't in the house. I'm not at all certain that Georgina wouldn't set him on me, if she could!'

'I'm sorry about all this,' said George's father. 'I wonder what the noise was that you heard. A log falling in the grate I expect. Now – what am I to do about that tiresome dog tonight? Go and take him outside, I suppose!'

'Leave him tonight,' said Mr Roland. 'I can hear noises upstairs – the others are awake by now! Don't let's make any more disturbance tonight.'

'Perhaps you are right,' said George's father, thankfully. He didn't at all want to tackle a defiant little girl and an angry big dog in the middle of a cold night!

The two men went to bed and slept. George did not sleep. The others had been awake when she got upstairs, and she had told them what had happened.

'George! You really are an idiot!' said Dick. 'After all, why shouldn't Mr Roland go down if he heard a noise! You went down! Now we shan't have darling old Tim in the house this cold weather!'

Anne began to cry. She didn't like hearing that the tutor she liked so much had been knocked down by Tim, and she hated hearing that Tim was to be punished.

'Don't be a baby,' said George. 'I'm not crying, and it's my dog!'

But, when everyone had settled down again in bed, and slept peacefully, George's pillow was very wet indeed. Tim crept up beside her and licked the salt tears off her cheek. He whined softly. Tim was always unhappy when his little mistress was sad.

from **FIVE GO ADVENTURING AGAIN**

A MISERABLE CHRISTMAS

'I DO THINK these Christmas holidays have been the worst we've ever had,' said Dick.

'Bad luck on George, coming to stay with us for Christmas – and then us all going down with those awful colds and coughs,' said Julian.

'Yes – and being in bed on Christmas Day was horrible,' said George. 'The worst of it was I couldn't eat anything. Fancy not being hungry on Christmas Day! I never thought that would happen to me!'

'Timmy was the only one of us who didn't get ill,' said Anne, patting him. 'You were a pet, Tim, when we were in bed. You divided your time between us nicely.'

'Woof!' said Timmy, rather solemnly. He hadn't been at all happy this Christmas. To have four of the Five in bed, coughing and sneezing, was quite unheard of!

'Well, anyhow, we're all up again,' said Dick. 'Though my legs don't really feel as if they belong to me yet!'

'Oh – do yours feel like that too?' asked George. 'I was quite worried about mine!'

'We all feel the same,' said Julian, 'but we shall be quite different in a day or two – now we're up. Anyway – we get back to school next week – so we'd better feel all right!'

Everyone groaned – and then coughed. 'That's the worst of this germ we've had, whatever it is,' said George. 'If we laugh – or speak loudly – or groan – we start coughing. I shall go completely mad if I don't get rid of my cough. It keeps me awake for hours at night!'

Anne went to the window. 'It's been snowing again,' she said. 'Not much – but it looks lovely. To think we might have been out in it all last week. I do think it's too bad to have holidays like this.'

George joined her at the window. A car drew up outside and a burly, merry-looking man got out and hurried up the steps to the front door.

'Here's the doctor,' said Anne. 'I bet he'll say we're all quite all right to go back to school next week!'

In a minute or two the door opened and the doctor came into the room, with the mother of Julian, Dick and Anne. She looked tired – and no wonder! Looking after four ill children and a most miserable dog over Christmas had not been an easy job!

'Well, here they are – all up and about now!' said the children's mother. 'They look pretty down in the mouth, don't they?'

'Oh – they'll soon perk up,' said Dr Drew, sitting down and looking at each of the four in turn.

'George looks the worst – not so strong as the others, I suppose.'

George went red with annoyance, and Dick chuckled. 'Poor George is the weakling of the family,' he said.

'She had the highest temperature, the worst cough, and the loudest groans, and she . . .'

But whatever else he was going to say was lost beneath the biggest cushion in the room, which an angry George had flung at him with all her might. Dick flung it back, and everyone began to laugh, George too. That set all the four coughing, of course, and the doctor put his hands to his ears.

'Will they be well enough to go to school, Doctor?' asked Mrs Barnard anxiously.

'Well, yes – they would – but they ought to get rid of those coughs first,' said the doctor. He looked out of the window at the snow. 'I wonder now – no – I don't suppose it's possible – but . . .'

'But what?' said Dick, pricking up his ears at once. 'Going to send us to Switzerland for a skiing holiday, Doc? Fine! Absolutely smashing!'

The doctor laughed. 'You're going too fast!' he said. 'No – I wasn't actually thinking of Switzerland – but perhaps somewhere hilly, not far from the sea. Somewhere really bracing, but not too cold – where the snow will lie, so that you can toboggan and ski, but without travelling as far as Switzerland. Switzerland is expensive, you know!'

'Yes. I suppose it is,' said Julian. 'No – we can't expect a holiday in Switzerland just because we've had beastly colds! But I must say a week somewhere would be jolly nice!'

'Oh yes!' said George, her eyes shining. 'It would really make up for these miserable holidays! Do you mean all by ourselves, Doctor? We'd love that.'

'Well, no – someone ought to be there, surely,' said Dr Drew. 'But that's up to your parents.'

'I think it's a jolly good idea,' said Julian. 'Mother – don't you think so? I'm sure you're longing to be rid of us for a while. You look worn out!'

His mother smiled. 'Well – if it's what you need – a short holiday somewhere to get rid of your coughs – you must have it. And I won't say that I shan't enjoy a little rest while you're enjoying yourselves having a good time! I'll talk it over with your father.'

'Woof!' said Timmy, looking inquiringly at the doctor, both ears pricked high.

'He says – he needs a rest somewhere too,' explained George. 'He wants to know if he can come with us.'

'Let's have a look at your tongue, Timmy, and give me your paw to feel if it's too hot or not,' said Dr Drew, gravely. He held out his hand, and Timmy obediently put his paw into it.

The four children laughed – and immediately began to cough again. How they coughed! The doctor shook his head at them. 'What a din! I shouldn't have made you laugh. Now I shan't be coming to see you again until just before you go back to school. I expect your mother will let me know when that day comes. Goodbye till then – and have a good time, wherever you go!'

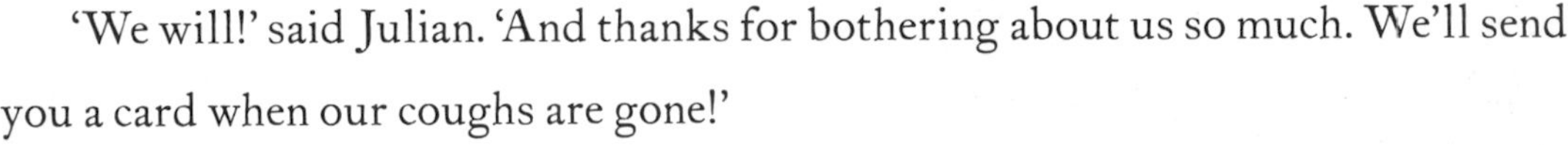

'We will!' said Julian. 'And thanks for bothering about us so much. We'll send you a card when our coughs are gone!'

As soon as Dr Drew had driven off in his car, there was a conference. 'We can go off somewhere, can't we, Mother?' said Dick, eagerly. 'The sooner the better! You must be tired to death of our coughs, night and day!'

'Yes. I think you must go somewhere for a few days,' said his mother. 'But the question is – where? You could go off to George's home, I suppose – Kirrin Cottage . . . but it's not high up . . . and besides, George's father would certainly not welcome four coughs like yours!'

'No. He'd go mad at once,' said George. 'He'd fling open his study door – and stride into our room – and shout "Who's mak—"'

But as George began to shout, she coughed – and that was the end of her little piece of acting! 'That's enough, George,' said her aunt. 'For goodness sake, go and get a drink of water.'

There was much debating about where they could go for a little while, and all the time they were talking the snow fell steadily. Dick went to the window, pleased. 'If only we could find a place high up on a hill, just as the doctor said – a place where we could use our toboggans, and our skis,' he said. 'Gosh, it makes me feel better already to think of it. I do hope this snow goes on and on.'

'I think I'd better ring up a travel agency and see if they can offer us something sensible,' said his mother. 'Maybe a summer camp set up on a hill would do – it would be empty now, and you could have a choice of a hut or a chalet or something.'

But all her telephoning came to nothing! 'No,' said the agencies. 'Sorry – we haven't anything to suggest. Our camps are all closed down now. No – we know of no winter ones in this country at all!'

And then, as so often happens, the problem was suddenly solved by somebody no one had thought of asking . . . Jenkins, the old man who helped in the garden! There was nothing for him to do that day except sweep a path through the snow.

He saw the children watching him from the window, grinned and came up to them.

'How are you?' he shouted. 'Would you like some apples? They've ripened nicely now, those late ones. Your mother said you weren't feeling like apples – or pears either. But maybe you're ready for some now.'

'Yes! We are!' shouted Julian, not daring to open the window in case his mother came in and was angry to see him standing with his head out in the cold. 'Bring them in, Jenkins. Come and talk to us!'

So old Jenkins came in, carrying a basket of ripe, yellow apples, and some plump, brown-yellow pears.

'And how are you now?' he said, in his soft Welsh voice, for he came from the Welsh mountains. 'You're pale, and thin too. Ah, it's the mountain air of Wales you want!'

He smiled all over his wrinkled brown face, handing round his basket. The children helped themselves to the fruit.

'Mountain air – that's what the doctor ordered!' said Julian, biting into a juicy pear. 'I suppose you don't know somewhere like that we could go to, do you, Jenkins?'

'Well, my aunt lets rooms in the summertime!' said Jenkins. 'And she's a good cook, my Aunt Glenys. But I don't know if she'd do it in the wintertime, what with the snow and all. Her farm's on the hillside, and the slope runs right down to the sea. A fine place it is in the summer – but there'll be nothing but snow there now.'

'But – it sounds exactly right,' said Anne, delighted. 'Doesn't it, Ju? Let's call Mother! Mother! Mother, where are you?'

Her mother came running in, afraid that one of the children was feeling ill again. She was most astonished to see old Jenkins there – and even more astonished to hear the four children pouring out what he had just told them. Timmy added a few excited barks, and Jenkins stood twirling his old hat, quite overcome.

The excitement made Julian and Dick cough distressingly. 'Now listen to me,' said their mother, firmly. 'Go straight upstairs and take another dose of your cough medicine. I'll talk to Jenkins and find out what all this is about. No – don't interrupt, Dick. GO!'

They went at once, and left their mother talking to the bewildered man. 'Blow this cough!' said Dick, pouring out his usual dose. 'Gosh. I hope Mother fixes up something with Jenkins's aunt. If I don't go off somewhere and lose this cough, I shall go mad – stark, staring mad!'

'I bet we'll go to his old aunt,' said Julian. 'That's if she'll take us. It's the kind of sudden idea that clicks – don't you think so?'

Julian was right. The idea did 'click'. His mother had actually met Jenkins's old aunt that spring, when she had come to visit her relations, and Jenkins had brought her proudly up to the house to introduce her. So when Dick and Julian went downstairs again, they were met with good news.

'I'm telephoning Jenkins's aunt, old Mrs Jones,' said their mother. 'And if she'll take you – well, off you can go in a day or two – coughs and all!'

from **FIVE GET INTO A FIX**

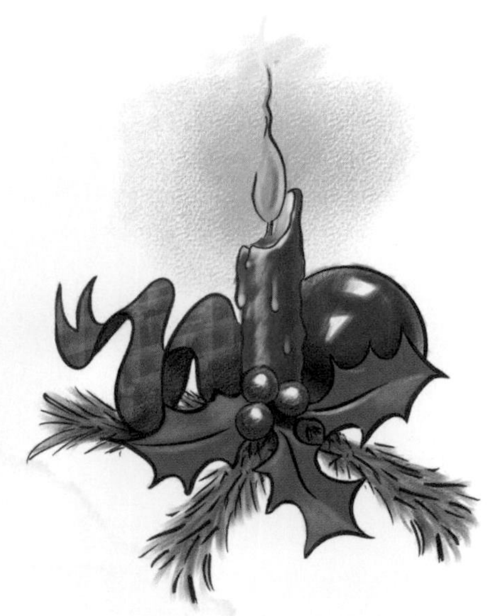

THE 'BIG, BIG HOLE'

During their holiday in Wales, the Five meet a shepherd's young daughter, called Aily. She has a pet lamb that follows her everywhere.

Next morning everyone was awake early. They had slept well, and were full of beans – and excited to think that an adventure lay ahead. To get into that old house, with its many secrets, would be marvellous!

Aily followed Julian about the room like a little dog. She wanted to have her breakfast on his knee, just as she had her supper the night before, and he let her.

He was ready to do anything she wanted – if only she would show them the way into Old Towers!

'We'd better set off pretty soon,' said Anne, looking out of the window. 'It's snowing pretty fast again – we don't want to get lost!'

'No. That's true. If Aily is going to take us across country, we shan't have the faintest idea where we're going in this heavy snow!' said Julian, rather anxiously.

'I'll just clear up a bit, then we'll go, shall we?' said Anne. 'Do we take any food with us, Ju?'

'We certainly do – all of us,' said Julian, at once. 'Goodness knows what time we'll get back to this hut. George, you make sandwiches with Anne, will you? And put in some bars of chocolate too, and some apples if there are any left.'

'And for pity's sake, let's remember our torches,' said Dick.

Aily watched while the sandwiches were made, and scraped up the bits that fell on the table to give to Dai, her small dog. The lamb frisked about, quite at home, getting into everyone's way. But nobody minded it – it was such a charming little long-leggitty creature!

At last all the sandwiches were made and put into two bags. The hut was cleared up and tidied, and the children got into their outdoor clothes.

'I think it would be easiest to toboggan down the slope, and halfway up Old

Towers' slope,' said Julian, looking out into the snow. 'It would take us ages to walk – and it's no good skiing, because Aily hasn't any skis – and couldn't use them if she had!'

'Oh yes – let's take the toboggans!' said George, pleased. 'What do we do with the lamb? Leave it here? And must we take Dai the dog, too?'

However, that was not for them to settle! Aily absolutely refused to go without her lamb and dog. She gathered them up into her arms, looking mutinous, when Julian suggested they should be left in the warm hut. Neither would she allow herself to be wrapped up warmly – and only consented to wear a scarf and a woollen hat because they happened to be exactly the same as Julian was wearing!

They set off at last. The snow was still falling, and Julian felt seriously doubtful whether they would be able to find their way down the hill and up the other slope without losing their sense of direction.

The toboggans were rather crowded! Julian and Dick were on the first one, with Aily and the lamb between them, and Anne and George were on the second one, with Timmy and Dai between them. George was at the front, and Anne had the awkward job of hanging on to both the dogs and keeping her balance too!

'I know we shall all roll off,' she said to George. 'Good gracious – I half wish we had waited a bit! The snow is falling very fast now!'

'Good thing!' called Julian. 'No one will spot us when we are near Old Towers – they won't be able to see a thing through this snow!'

Julian's toboggan shot off down the snowy slope. It gathered speed, and the boys gasped in delight at the pace. Aily clung to Julian's back, half frightened, and the lamb stared with astonished eyes, not daring to move from its place, squashed in between Aily and Julian!

Whoooooooosh! Down the slope to the bottom, and up the opposite slope, gradually slowing down! Julian's toboggan came to a stop, and then, not far behind, came George's, slowing down too. George got out and dragged her toboggan over

to Julian.

'Well,' she said, her face glowing, 'what do we do now? Wasn't that a wonderful run?'

'Wonderful!' said Julian. 'I only wish we could have a few more! Did you like that, Aily?'

'No,' said Aily, pulling her woollen cap to exactly the same angle that Julian wore his. 'No. It makes my nose cold, so cold.'

She cupped her hand over her nose to make it warm. George laughed.

'Fancy complaining about a cold nose when she's hardly wearing anything on her skinny little body – you'd think the whole of her would feel cold – not just her nose!'

'Aily – do you know where the big hole is?' asked Julian, looking about in the snow. The snowflakes were quite big now, and nothing that was more than a few yards away could be seen. Aily stood there, her feet sinking into the snow. She looked all round, and Julian felt certain that she was going to say that she didn't know which way to go, in this thick snow. Even he was rather doubtful which was the way back up the hill!

But Aily was like a dog. She had a sure sense of direction, and could go from one place to another on a dark night or in the snow without any difficulty at all!

She nodded.

'Aily know – Dai know, too.'

She walked a few steps, but her feet sank into the snow about her ankles, and her thin shoes were soon soaked through.

'She'll get her feet frostbitten,' said Dick. 'Better put her on one of the toboggans and pull her, Ju. Pity we didn't have any snow-boots small enough to lend her. I say – this is a bit of a crazy expedition, isn't it! I hope to goodness Aily knows where's she's taking us. I haven't the foggiest idea at the moment which is east or west, north or south!'

'Wait – I've got a compass in one of my pockets,' said Julian, and did a lot of digging in his clothes. At last he pulled out a small compass. He looked at it.

'That's south,' he said, pointing, 'so that's where Old Towers Hill is – south is directly opposite our hut; we know that because the sun shone straight in at our front windows. I reckon we walk this way, then – due south.'

'Let's see which way Aily points,' said Dick. He set her on his toboggan, and wrapped her scarf more closely round her. 'Now – which way, Aily?'

Aily at once pointed due south. Everyone was most impressed.

'That's right,' said Julian. 'Come on, Dick – I'll pull Aily's toboggan, you can pull the girls' for them.'

They all set off up the rest of the slope of Old Towers Hill, Aily on the toboggan with Dai and Fany the lamb, and Timmy sitting in state on George's toboggan, the girls walking behind. Timmy was enjoying himself. He didn't like the way his legs went down into the snow when he tried to run – it was much easier to sit on the toboggan and be pulled along!

'Lazy thing!' said George, and Timmy wagged his tail, not caring a bit what anyone said!

Julian looked at his compass as he went, and walked due south for some time. Then Aily gave a call, and pointed to the right.

'That way, that way,' she said.

'She wants us to go westwards now,' said Julian, stopping. 'I wonder if she's right. By my reckoning we're going dead straight for Old Towers now – but we shall be going up the hill to the right of it, if we go her way.'

'That way, that way,' repeated Aily, imperiously, and Dai barked as if to say she was right!

'Better follow her way,' said Dick. 'She seems so jolly certain of it.'

So Julian swerved to the right a little, and the others followed. They went a good way up the steep hill, and Julian began to pant.

'Is it far now?' he asked Aily, who was petting her lamb, and apparently taking

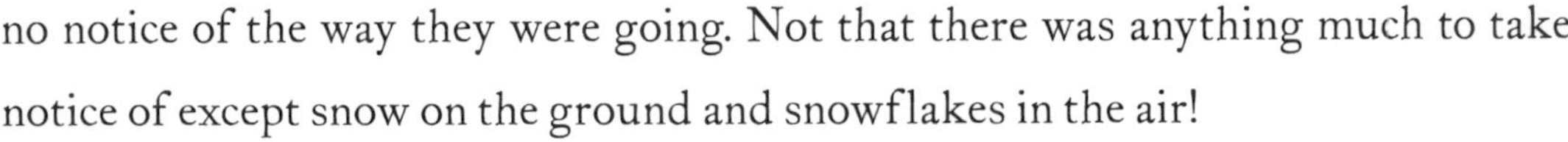

no notice of the way they were going. Not that there was anything much to take notice of except snow on the ground and snowflakes in the air!

Aily looked up. Then she pointed again, a little more to the right, and said something in Welsh, nodding her head.

'Well – it looks as if we're getting near this place of hers – this "big, big hole", whatever it is,' said Julian, and on he went.

In about a minute Aily suddenly leapt off the toboggan and stood there, looking round with a frown.

'Here,' she said. 'Big hole here.'

'Well – it may be – but I'd like to see it a bit more clearly, Aily,' said Julian. Aily began to scrape down through the snow, and Timmy and Dai obligingly went to help her, imagining that she was after rabbits or a hidden hare.

'I'm afraid the poor kid's led us on a wild-goose chase,' said Dick. 'Why should there be a big hole here?'

Timmy and Aily had now got down through the snow to the buried clumps of heather that grew all over the slopes of the mountains in that district. Julian could see the clumps sticking up, stiff and wiry, in the clearing that Aily and the dogs had made.

'Timmy – you take Timmy!' said Aily, suddenly to George. 'He'll fall down, down – he'll fall like Dai one day – down, down!'

'I say! I believe she's looking for an old pot-hole!' said Dick, suddenly. 'You know – those strange holes that are sometimes found on moors – sudden holes that drop right down underground. They're called dean-holes I think, in some places. We found one once on Kirrin Island – don't you remember?'

'Oh yes – that was in the heather too!' said George, remembering. 'And it led to a cave below, by the seashore! That's what Aily meant by a big, big hole! A pot-hole on the moors! Timmy – for goodness sake come away – you may drop right down it!'

Timmy very nearly did go down the hole! George just caught his collar in time! But Dai was wary – he had fallen down once before!

'Hole!' said Aily, pleased. 'Big, big hole! Aily find for you!'

'Well – certainly you've found your hole – but how does it get us into Old Towers?' said Dick. Aily didn't understand. She knelt there, looking down at the hole she had uncovered under the heather and the snow.

'I must say that was a marvellous feat,' said Julian. 'Coming straight to this place and finding the hole when she couldn't see a thing through the falling snow. She really is as good as a dog. Good little Aily bach!'

Aily gave one of her sudden smiles, and slipped her hand in Julian's.

'Go down, yes?' she said. 'Aily show way?'

'Well – we'd better go down if it's possible,' said Julian, not much liking the idea, for he could see nothing but darkness inside the hole, and had no idea of what lay below.

Fany the lamb was tired of waiting about. She gave a little leap to the edge of the big, round hole, and then put her small head in. She kicked up her heels – and was gone!

'She's jumped into the hole!' said George, amazed. 'Here, wait, Aily – you can't jump too – you'll hurt yourself!'

But Aily slithered into the hole, then let herself go.

'Aily here,' came a small voice from below. 'You come quick!'

from **FIVE GET INTO A FIX**

MAKE YOUR OWN WRAPPING PAPER!

Do you have a big pile of presents to wrap up for Christmas, just like the Famous Five in the story called *Happy Christmas, Five!*? Have you thought about making your own wrapping paper? It's unique, beautiful and cheaper than shop-bought! You can even personalise it to make it fit the recipient of the present. Here are a few ideas for you to try:

GET A GOLD STAR

Use plain black paper and draw on your own stars with a gold marker or gel pen.
Quick, easy to do and looks lovely!

STAMP ON YOUR OWN DESIGN

Take brown parcel (or kraft) paper and decorate with your own stamped designs. You can use picture or shape stampers, particularly if you have some with Christmas themes, or use letter stampers to spell out names or messages.

USE POTATO PRINTING

Cut a potato in half.
Carve out a simple shape on one cut surface (e.g. a Christmas tree or star).
Dip in poster paint or use a stamper ink pad, and print on to your paper.
Leave to dry before wrapping your presents.

PAPER FOR PUZZLERS

Using plain white paper, carefully write or stamp a word search grid on the paper. Create words to find that spell out a message such as 'Merry Christmas to you'. Then you can either highlight the special words or leave them for the recipient of the present to find, so they get a challenge as well as a gift for Christmas! This is perfect for people who like to puzzle things out, as Julian does.

WRAPPING IN MAPPING

If you or someone you know has old maps that are no longer in use, they make very interesting and unusual gift wrap. Just make sure they're no longer wanted before you cut them up! This would make an ideal design for presents for adventurers and explorers like George.

LACE AND SNOWFLAKES

Stick white doilies over any plain coloured paper for an extra-pretty lacy finish to your wrapping that Anne would love!

JUST FOR LAUGHS

Save up your old comics, and choose pages to use as brightly coloured gift wrap, carefully removing the staples first. Dick would love to have this jolly paper round his Christmas presents.

GET TO KNOW GEORGE

Don't try to call George by her proper name, Georgina. She hates it! She wishes that she were a boy and will never wear dresses. When Julian, Dick and Anne first meet their cousin she is a fierce, hot-tempered girl who is often moody and sulky. As she gets to know her three cousins she begins to change, gradually realising that things are much more fun if she shares them.

George has many excellent qualities. She has a kind heart, is loyal to her friends and is absolutely truthful. She loves outdoor activities and is a wonderful swimmer, rope thrower and climber. She has 'the sharpest ears of the lot' and we are told that 'no one had such good eyes as George'.

George has a hot temper, but she is brave. The only time she ever shows any sign of fear is when Timmy is in danger. Crooks and villains had better watch out if they make her angry or threaten Timmy, for sparks are sure to fly before the end of the adventure.

Other people say

Who can stop George doing what she wants to!

If a person doesn't like dogs, especially a dog like our Timothy, then there really must be something wrong with him.

George says

I don't make friends with people just because they're my cousins, or something silly like that. I only make friends with people if I like them.

FEASTS with THE FAMOUS FIVE

WELL DONE, FAMOUS FIVE

'Nice to be together again,' said Julian. 'All five of us!'

George nodded. 'Yes, Timmy's thrilled too. Aren't you, Tim?'

Timmy the dog barked, and laid his big head on George's knee, and she patted him.

All the Five were on the top of Kirrin Hill, looking at the wide spread of country stretched out below them. Anne was handing out the picnic food, and Dick passed it round.

Timmy raised his head at once, and sniffed. Would there be anything for him?

'Of course, Timmy,' said Anne. 'A bone – and two big dog biscuits.'

'As well as a good part of our own sandwiches and buns, I expect,' said Dick. 'No, Tim – that pile's mine – and I'm not going to exchange my biscuits for yours!'

'What a wonderful view we've got from here,' said Julian, beginning to munch his sandwich. 'We can see for miles and miles all round us.'

'Well – not much is happening,' said Anne, 'except that those sheep are rambling around that field, and those cows are doing what they always do – eat, eat, eat all day long – although if I had to eat nothing but grass, I'd soon stop!'

'Can't see a soul about,' said Dick, lazily. 'I suppose it's everyone's dinner-time. Now, why can't something exciting happen, just to give us a bit of interest while we're eating! We've had so many adventures that I'm beginning to feel quite cheated if one doesn't turn up as soon as we're together again!'

'Oh, for goodness sake, don't wish for an adventure today!' said Anne. 'I like a bit of peace. I don't want to choke with excitement when I'm eating these delicious sandwiches! What has Aunt Fan put into them?'

'A bit of everything in the larder, I should think,' said George. 'Get away, Tim – don't breathe all over me like that!'

'What's that moving right away over there – along the side of that hill?' asked Dick, suddenly. 'Is it cows?'

Everyone looked. 'Too far away to see,' said George. 'Can't be cows, though – they don't move like cows – cows walk so slowly.'

'Well, they must be horses then,' said Julian.

'But who'd have so many horses out for exercise round here?' said George. 'All the horses are farm horses – they'd be working in the fields, not trotting in a row across a hillside.'

'It must be a riding school, idiot,' said Dick. 'If we had our binoculars, we'd see a lot of nicely behaved little girls from some nearby school cantering along on their nicely behaved horses!'

'I did bring my binoculars – didn't you notice?' said George, rummaging about behind her. 'I put them down here somewhere – ah, here they are. Want them, Dick?'

Dick took them and put them to his eyes.

'Yes – it's a line of horses – about six – wonderful ones, too. But it's not girls who are riding them – it's boys – stable boys, I think.'

'Oh, of course – I forgot,' said George. 'They're wonderful racing horses from Lord Daniron's stable – they have to be exercised each day. Can you see a very big horse in the line, Dick? A magnificent creature – he's called Thunder-Along, and he's the most valuable horse in the country – so they say!'

Dick was now examining the horses with much interest, holding the binoculars to his eyes.

'They're lovely horses – and yes, I think I can see the one you mean, George. A great horse with a wonderful head – he's the first one of all.'

'Let me see,' said George.

Dick held on to the binoculars. 'No. Half a mo. Hey – something's happening!'

'What is it?' said George.

'Something seemed to rush straight across in front of Thunder-Along – was it a fox or a dog? Oh, he's rearing up in fright, he's in quite a panic. He . . .' Then Dick suddenly shouted, 'He's off! He's thrown his groom – yes, he's on the ground, hurt, I think – and he's bolting! Oh no – he'll kill himself.'

A silence fell on the Five. Even Timmy was quiet, staring in the same direction as the others. George made as if to snatch her binoculars away from Dick, but he dodged, gluing them to his eyes.

'Don't lose sight of the horse, Dick, keep the binoculars on him,' said Julian, urgently. 'He's the finest horse this country has. Watch him – watch where he goes! We may be the only people who can see the way he takes.'

'All right, all right,' said Dick, impatiently. 'Don't jog my arm, Anne. Yes – there he goes – he's scared! He's still bolting at top speed – I hope he doesn't run into a tree! No, he just missed that one. Oh, now he's come to a gate – a high gate . . .'

The others had now lost sight of the horse and were hanging on to every word of Dick's.

Timmy was so excited that he began to bark, sensing the general excitement. George shushed him, fearing to lose something that Dick said.

'He's over the gate – what a jump, oh what a jump! Now he's galloping down the road – I can't see him – yes, there he is again – he's come to the stream – he's over it, cleared it beautifully – away he goes, up Rilling Hill – now he's going more slowly – he must be absolutely puffed. He's gone into a field of corn – the farmer won't like that!' said Dick.

He continued, 'And now – he must be lying down in the corn! I can't see him any more!'

George snatched the binoculars from Dick – no, she couldn't see him either. She switched them to the hillside where the horses had been exercising.

What a commotion! The grooms were talking excitedly, pointing here and there, evidently at a loss to know where Thunder-Along had gone!

'I'm afraid this is the end of our picnic,' said Julian. 'As long as Thunder-Along is in the field of corn, resting, he's safe – but if he goes off again, anything may happen!'

He added, 'We've got to report our news at once – and Dick, you'd better bike as fast as you can to that cornfield. Maybe the horse will still be there.'

Dick ran to where he had left his bike, and leapt on it.

The others went to theirs, too, and soon they were riding off to Kirrin to report their news to the police, who would at once get in touch with the stables.

Dick planned out his way as he went. What would be the best way to get quickly to Rilling Hill? He soon made up his mind, and cycled along at top speed. It seemed a very long way – but at last he was cycling up the hill to where he hoped to find the field of corn. He was so out of breath that he had to get off his bike and walk.

He came to the field gate and looked in cautiously at the corn. He could see no horse at all – and no wonder, for he would be lying down!

'I'll have to tread in carefully,' thought Dick. 'I can see the way he trod – where the corn's flattened.' So in he went – only to hear a furious voice yelling at him from the gate behind him.

'Come out of that corn! Come out at once!' It was the farmer, red with anger. Dick didn't like to yell back, in case he frightened the horse.

So he pointed urgently into the field and went carefully on.

'You wait!' yelled the farmer. 'I'll get the police on to you!'

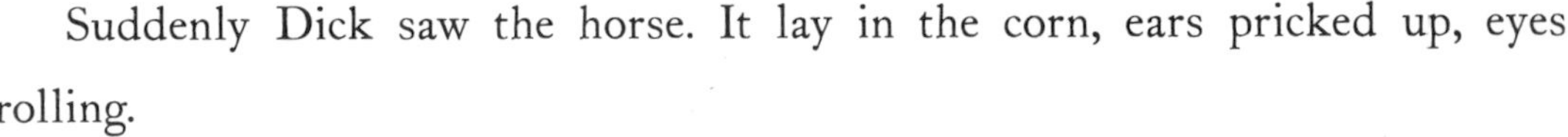

Suddenly Dick saw the horse. It lay in the corn, ears pricked up, eyes rolling.

Dick stopped. 'Well, old beauty?' he said. 'Well, you magnificent thing! Thunder-Along! Do you know your name? Poor boy, how frightened you were! Come now, come! You're safe – come along with me!'

To his surprise and delight the great horse stood up and flicked his ears to and fro, watching Dick carefully. Then he whinnied a little, and stepped towards him.

The boy took hold of the reins gently, and dared to rub the velvety nose. Then he led the horse carefully out of the corn.

The farmer stood staring in amazement at the magnificent creature.

'But – but, isn't that Lord Daniron's horse, Thunder-Along?' he said, almost in a whisper. 'Did he bolt?'

Dick nodded his head. 'Keep my bike for me, will you?' he said. 'I must take the horse while he's quiet. I expect as soon as the owners know where he is, they'll send a horsebox. I'll lead him up and down the lane for a little, till they come.'

It wasn't long before a great horsebox drove slowly up the lane, and Thunder-Along's own groom came to pet him and lead him quietly into it.

He ran his eyes over the horse carefully.

'No damage done!' he said. 'Thank goodness you had binoculars with you, boy, and saw where he went. You did well to get him!'

As soon as the horsebox had gone down the hill, Dick jumped on his bike and rode away.

He soon met the others, cycling towards him, anxious to know what had happened. Timmy was running beside them.

'The horse was all right. I got him, and there's not a scratch on him!' said Dick. 'What a bit of luck we had this morning, looking through your binoculars, George! What do you say, Timmy?'

'Woof!' said Timmy, agreeing as usual. 'Woof!'

'He says it's the kind of thing that would happen to the Famous Five!' said George.

And, of course, she was quite right!

A DAY ON THE ISLAND

The children hardly knew where they were the next day when they woke up. The sun was pouring into the cave entrance, and fell first of all on George's sleeping face. It awoke her and she lay half-dozing, wondering why her bed felt rather less soft than usual.

'But I'm not in my bed – I'm on Kirrin Island, of course!' she thought suddenly to herself. She sat up and gave Anne a punch. 'Wake up, sleepy-head! We're on the island!'

Soon they were all awake rubbing the sleep from their eyes. 'I think I'm going to get heather today for my bed, after all,' said Anne. 'The sand feels soft at first, but it gets hard after a bit.'

The others agreed that they would all get heather for their beds, set on the sand, with rugs for covering. Then they would have really fine beds.

'It's fun to live in a cave,' said Dick. 'Fancy having a fine cave like this on our island, as well as a castle and dungeons! We are really very lucky.'

'I feel sticky and dirty,' said Julian. 'Let's go and have a bathe before we have breakfast. Then cold ham, bread, pickles and marmalade for me!'

'We shall be cold after our bathe,' said George. 'We'd better light my little stove and put the kettle on to boil while we're bathing. Then we can make some hot cocoa when we come back shivering!'

'Oh yes,' said Anne, who had never boiled anything on such a tiny stove before. 'Do let's. I'll fill the kettle with water from one of the containers. What shall we do for milk?'

'There's a tin of milk somewhere in the pile,' said Julian. 'We can open that. Where's the tin-opener?'

It was not to be found, which was most exasperating. But at last Julian discovered it in his pocket, so all was well.

The little stove was filled with methylated spirit, and lit. The kettle was filled and set on top. Then the children went off to bathe.

'Look! There's a simply marvellous pool in the middle of those rocks over there!' called Julian, pointing. 'We've never spotted it before. Golly, it's like a small swimming pool, made specially for us!'

'Kirrin Swimming Pool, twenty pence a dip!' said Dick. Free to the owners, though! Come on – it looks gorgeous! And see how the waves keep washing over the top of the rocks and splashing into the pool. Couldn't be better!'

It really was a lovely rock pool, deep, clear and not too cold. The children enjoyed themselves thoroughly, splashing about and swimming and floating. George tried a dive off one of the rocks, and went in beautifully.

'George can do anything in the water,' said Anne, admiringly. 'I wish I could dive and swim like George. But I never shall.'

'We can see the old wreck nicely from here,' said Julian, coming out of the water. 'Blow! We didn't bring any towels.'

'We'll use one of the rugs, turn and turn about,' said Dick. 'I'll go and fetch the thinnest one. I say – do you remember that trunk we saw in the wreck yesterday? Odd, wasn't it?'

'Yes, very odd,' said Julian. 'I don't understand it. We'll have to keep a watch on the wreck and see who comes to collect the trunk.'

'I suppose the smugglers – if they are smugglers – will come slinking round this side of the island and quietly send off a boat to the wreck,' said George, drying herself vigorously. 'Well, we'd better keep a strict lookout, and see if anything appears on the sea out there in the way of a small steamer, boat or ship.'

'Yes. We don't want them to spot us,' said Dick. 'We shan't find out anything if they see us and are warned. They'd at once give up coming to the island. I vote we each of us take turns at keeping a lookout, so that we can spot anything at once and get under cover.'

'Good idea!' said Julian. 'Well, I'm dry, but not very warm. Let's race to the cave, and get that hot drink. And breakfast – golly, I could eat a whole chicken and probably a duck as well, to say nothing of a turkey.'

The others laughed. They all felt the same. They raced off to the cave, running over the sand and climbing over a few rocks, then down to the cave-beach and into the big entrance, still splashed with sunshine.

The kettle was boiling away merrily, sending a cloud of steam up from its tin spout. 'Get the ham out and a loaf of bread, and that jar of pickles we brought,' ordered Julian. 'I'll open the tin of milk. George, you take the tin of cocoa and that jug, and make enough for all of us.'

'I'm so terribly happy,' said Anne, as she sat at the entrance to the cave, eating her breakfast. 'It's a lovely feeling. It's simply gorgeous being on our island like this, all by ourselves, able to do what we like.'

from **FIVE RUN AWAY TOGETHER**

FOOD FROM THE FARM

NEXT MORNING, while Anne cleared up the breakfast things with George, and Dick went off to the farm to buy whatever the farmer's wife had ready for him, Julian took the field-glasses and sat on the ledge to watch for Nobby to go out on the lake in his boat.

Dick sauntered along, whistling. The farmer's wife was delighted to see him, and showed him two big baskets full of delicious food.

'Slices of ham I've cured myself,' she said, lifting up the white cloth that covered one of the baskets. 'And a pot of brawn I've made. Keep it in a cool place. And some fresh lettuces and radishes I pulled myself this morning early. And some more tomatoes.'

'How gorgeous!' said Dick, eyeing the food in delight. 'Just the kind of things we love! Thanks awfully, Mrs Mackie. What's in the other basket?'

'Eggs, butter, milk, and a tin of shortbread I've baked,' said Mrs Mackie. 'You should do all right till tomorrow, the four of you! And in that paper there is a bone for the dog.'

How much do I owe you?' asked Dick. He paid his bill and took up the baskets. Mrs Mackie slipped a bag into his pocket.

'Just a few home-made sweets,' she said. That was her little present. Dick grinned at her.

'Well, I won't offer to pay you for them because I'm afraid of that rolling pin of yours,' he said. 'But thank you very, very much.'

from **FIVE GO OFF IN A CARAVAN**

UP ON THE MOORS

THEY STOPPED about half past twelve for lunch. Mr Luffy had indeed provided sandwiches for everyone. And remarkably fine ones they were too, made the evening before by Mrs Luffy.

'Cucumber, dipped in vinegar! Ham and lettuce! Egg! Sardine! Oooh, Mr Luffy, your sandwiches are much nicer than ours,' said Anne, beginning on two together, one cucumber and the other ham and lettuce.

They were all very hungry. Timmy had a bit from everyone, usually the last bite, and watched each sandwich eagerly till his turn came. Mr Luffy didn't seem to understand that Timmy had to have the last bite of any sandwich, so Timmy simply took it out of his hand, much to his surprise.

'A clever dog,' he said, and patted him. 'Knows what he wants and takes it. Very clever.'

That pleased George, of course. She thought that Timmy was the cleverest dog in the world, and indeed it did seem like it at times. He understood every word she said to him, every pat, every stroke, every gesture. He would be much, much better at keeping an eye on the four children and guarding them than forgetful Mr Luffy.

They drank ginger beer and then ate some ripe plums. Timmy wouldn't have any plums, but he licked up some spilt ginger beer. Then he snuffed up a few odd crumbs and went to drink at a little stream nearby.

The party set off again in the car. Anne fell asleep. Dick gave an enormous yawn and fell asleep too. George wasn't sleepy and nor was Timmy, but Julian was. He didn't dare to take his eye off the speedometer, though, because Mr Luffy seemed to be very much inclined to speed along too fast again, after his good lunch.

from **FIVE GO OFF TO CAMP**

A SMASHING DINNER

They all sat down to dinner. There was a big meat pie, a cold ham, salad, potatoes in their jackets, and home-made pickles. It really was difficult to know what to choose.

'Have some of both,' said Mrs Andrews, cutting the meat pie. 'Begin with the pie and go on with the ham. That's the best of living on a farm, you know – you do get plenty to eat.'

After the first course there were plums and thick cream, or jam tarts and the same cream. Everyone tucked in hungrily.

'I've never had such a lovely dinner in my life,' said Anne, at last. 'I wish I could eat some more but I can't. It was super, Mrs Andrews.'

'Smashing,' said Dick. That was his favourite word these holidays. 'Absolutely smashing.'

'Woof,' said Timmy, agreeing. He had had a fine plateful of meaty bones, biscuits and gravy, and he had licked up every crumb and every drop. Now he felt he would like to have a snooze in the sun and not do a thing for the rest of the day.

The children felt rather like that, too. Mrs Andrews handed them a chocolate each and sent them out of doors. 'You go and have a rest now,' she said. 'Talk to Jock. He doesn't get enough company of his own age in the holidays. You can stay on to tea, if you like.'

'Oh thanks,' said everyone, although they all felt that they wouldn't even be able to manage a biscuit.

from **FIVE GO OFF TO CAMP**

TIME FOR AN ICE CREAM

THE MORNING was very warm. Soon the children began to feel wet with perspiration. They had sweaters on and they took them off, stuffing them in their baskets. George looked more like a boy than ever, with her short curly hair blown up by the wind. All of them wore shorts and thin jerseys except Julian, who had on jeans. He rolled up the sleeves of his jersey, and the others did the same.

They covered mile after mile, enjoying the sun and the wind. Timmy galloped beside them, untiring, his long pink tongue hanging out. He ran on the grassy edge of the road when there was one. He really was a very sensible dog!

They stopped at a tiny village called Manlington-Tovey. It had only one general store, but it sold practically everything – or seemed to! 'Hope it sells ginger beer!' said Julian. 'My tongue's hanging out like Timmy's!'

The little shop sold lemonade, orangeade, lime juice, grapefruit juice and ginger beer. It was really difficult to choose which to have. It also sold ice creams, and soon the children were sitting drinking ginger beer and lime juice mixed, and eating delicious ices.

'Timmy must have an ice,' said George. 'He does so love them. Don't you, Timmy?'

'Woof,' said Timmy, and gulped his ice down in two big, gurgly licks.

'It's really a waste of ice creams to give them to Timmy,' said Anne. 'He hardly has time to taste them, he gobbles them so. No, Timmy, get down. I'm going to finish up every single bit of mine, and there won't be even a lick for you!'

Timmy went off to drink from a bowl of water that the shopwoman had put down for him. He drank and he drank, then he flopped down, panting.

The children took a bottle of ginger beer each with them when they went off again. They meant to have it with their lunch. Already they were beginning to think with pleasure of eating the sandwiches put up into neat packets for them.

Anne saw some cows pulling at the grass in a meadow as they passed. 'It must be awful to be a cow and eat nothing but tasteless grass,' she called to George. 'Think what a cow misses – never tastes an egg-and-lettuce sandwich, never eats a chocolate eclair, never has a boiled egg – and can't even drink a glass of ginger beer! Poor cows!'

George laughed. 'You do think of silly things, Anne,' she said. 'Now you've made me want my lunch all the more – talking about egg sandwiches and ginger beer! I know Mother made us egg sandwiches – and sardine ones too.'

'It's no good,' chimed in Dick, leading the way into a little copse, his bicycle wobbling dangerously. 'It's no good – we can't go another inch if you girls are going to jabber about food all the time. Julian, what about lunch?'

It was a lovely picnic, that first one in the copse. There were clumps of primroses all round, and from somewhere nearby came the sweet scent of hidden violets. A thrush was singing madly on a hazel tree, with two chaffinches calling 'pink-pink' every time he stopped.

'Band and decorations laid on,' said Julian, waving his hand towards the singing birds and the primroses. 'Very nice too. We just want a waiter to come and present us with a menu!'

A rabbit lolloped near, its big ears standing straight up inquiringly. 'Ah – the waiter!' said Julian, at once. 'What have you to offer us today, Bunny? A nice rabbit pie?'

The rabbit scampered off at top speed. It had caught the smell of Timmy nearby and was panic-stricken. The children laughed, because it seemed as if it was the mention of rabbit pie that had sent it away. Timmy stared at the disappearing rabbit, but made no move to go after it.

from **FIVE GET INTO TROUBLE**

ALL TOGETHER AGAIN

A wonderful smell came creeping into the little dining-room, followed by the inn-woman carrying a large tray. On it was a steaming tureen of porridge, a bowl of golden syrup, a jug of very thick cream and a dish of bacon and eggs, all piled high on crisp brown toast. Little mushrooms were on the same dish.

'It's like magic!' and Anne, staring. 'Just the very things I longed for!'

'Toast, marmalade and butter to come, and the coffee and hot milk,' said the woman, busily setting everything out. 'And if you want any more bacon and eggs, just ring the bell.'

'Too good to be true!' said Dick, looking at the table. 'For goodness sake, help yourselves quickly, girls, or I shall forget my manners and grab.'

It was a wonderful breakfast – extra wonderful because they were all so ravenously hungry. There wasn't a word said as they spooned up their porridge and cream, sweetened with golden syrup. Timmy had a dishful too – he loved porridge, though he didn't like the syrup – it made his whiskers sticky!

'I feel better,' said Anne, looking at the porridge dish. 'The thing is – shall I have some more porridge and risk not enjoying my bacon and eggs so much – or shall I go straight on with bacon and eggs?'

'A difficult question,' said Dick. 'And one that I am faced with too. On the whole I think I'll go on with bacon and eggs – we can always have more of those if we want to – and those little mushrooms really do make my mouth water! Aren't we greedy? But how can anyone help that when they're so hungry?'

from **FIVE ON A HIKE TOGETHER**

TEA AT THE FARMHOUSE

They went for a walk in the afternoon, but didn't quite get to the sea. They saw it from a hill, sparkling blue in the distance. Little white yachts dotted the blue water like far-off swans with wings outspread. They had tea at a farmhouse, watched by a couple of big-eyed farm children.

'Do you want to take some of my home-made jam with you?' asked the farmer's jolly, red-faced wife, when they paid her for their tea.

'Oh, yes, rather!' said Dick. 'And I suppose you couldn't sell us some of that fruit cake? We're camping in caravans in Faynights Field, just opposite the castle – so we're having picnic meals each day.'

'Yes, you can have a whole cake,' said the farmer's wife. 'I did my baking yesterday, so there's plenty. And would you like some ham? And I've some good pickled onions too.'

This was wonderful! They bought all the food very cheaply indeed, and carried it home gladly. Dick took off the lid of the pickled onions halfway back to the caravans, and sniffed.

'Better than any scent!' he said. 'Have a sniff, George.'

It didn't stop at sniffs, of course. Everyone took out a large pickled onion – except Timmy who backed away at once. Onions were one thing he really couldn't bear. Dick put back the lid.

'I think somebody else ought to carry the onions, not Dick,' said Anne. 'There won't be many left by the time we reach our caravans!'

from **FIVE HAVE A WONDERFUL TIME**

TREMANNON FARM

'We'll bike to the sea as soon as we can,' said Dick, trying to flatten the few hairs that would stick up straight on the top of his head. 'There are caves on this coast. We'll explore them. I wonder if Mrs Penruthlan would give us picnic lunches so that we can go off for the day when we want to.'

'Sure to,' said Julian. 'She's a pet. I've never felt so welcome in my life. Are we ready? Come on down, then. I'm beginning to feel very empty indeed.'

The high tea that awaited them was truly magnificent. A huge ham gleaming as pink as Timmy's tongue; a salad fit for a king. In fact, as Dick said, fit for several kings, it was so enormous. It had in it everything that anyone could possibly want.

'Lettuce, tomatoes, onions, radishes, mustard and cress, carrot grated up – this is carrot, isn't it, Mrs Penruthlan?' said Dick. 'And lashings of hard-boiled eggs.'

There was an enormous tureen of new potatoes, all gleaming with melted butter, scattered with parsley. There was a big bottle of home-made salad cream.

'Look at that cream cheese, too,' marvelled Dick, quite overcome. 'And that fruit cake. And are those drop-scones, or what? Are we supposed to have something of everything, Mrs Penruthlan?'

'Oh, yes,' said the plump little woman, smiling at Dick's pleasure. 'And there's a cherry tart made with our own cherries, and our own cream with it. I know what hungry children are. I've had seven of my own, all married and gone away. So I have to make do with other people's when I can get them.'

'I'm jolly glad you happened to get hold of *us*,' said Dick, beginning on ham and salad. 'Well, we'll keep you busy, Mrs Penruthlan. We've all got big appetites!'

'Ah, I've not met any children yet that could eat like mine,' said Mrs Penruthlan, sounding really sorry. 'Same as I've not met any man that can eat like Mr Penruthlan. He's a fine eater, he is. He'll be in soon.'

'I hope we shall leave enough for him,' said Anne, looking at the ham and the half-empty salad dish. 'No wonder my uncle's friend, the man who came to stay here, went away as fat as butter, Mrs Penruthlan.'

'Oh, the poor man!' said their hostess, who was now filling up their glasses with rich, creamy milk. 'Thin as my husband's old rake, he was, and all his bones showing and creaking. He said "No" to this and "No" to that, but I took no notice of him at all. If he didn't eat his dinner, I'd take his tray away and tidy it up, and then in ten minutes I'd take it back again and say: "Dinner-time, sir, and I hope you're hungry!" And he'd start all over again, and maybe that time he'd really tuck in!'

'But didn't he know you'd already taken him his dinner tray once?' said Julian, astonished. 'Goodness, he must have been a dreamer.'

'I took his tray in three times once,' said Mrs Penruthlan. 'So you be careful in case I do the same kind of thing to you!'

'I should love it!' grinned Julian. 'Yes, please, I'd like some more ham. *And* more salad.'

from **FIVE GO DOWN TO THE SEA**

PREPARING FOR THE SHOW

Mrs Penruthlan came to see the barn now that it was almost ready for the show the next night. She looked red and excited. This was a grand time for her, the Barnies in her barn, the villagers all coming up the next night, a grand supper to be held afterwards. What an excitement!

She was very busy in her kitchen, cooking, cooking, cooking! Her enormous larder was already full of the most appetising-looking pies, tarts, hams and cheeses.

The children took turns at looking into it and sniffing in delight. Mrs Penruthlan laughed at them and shooed them out.

'You'll have to help me tomorrow,' she said. 'Shelling peas, scraping potatoes, stringing beans, picking currants and raspberries, and you'll find hundreds of wild strawberries in the copse too, which can go to add a flavour to the fruit salad.'

'We shall love to help,' said Anne. 'All this is grand fun! But surely you aren't going to do all the supper single-handed, Mrs Penruthlan?'

'Oh, one or two of the villagers will stay behind to help me serve it,' said the plump little farmer's wife, who looked as happy as could be in the midst of so much hard work. 'Anyway, I'll be up at five o'clock tomorrow morning. I'll have plenty of time!'

'You'd better go to bed early tonight then!' said George.

'We all will,' said Mrs Penruthlan. 'We'll be up early and abed late tomorrow, and we'll need some sleep tonight. It's no trouble to get Mr Penruthlan to bed early. He's always ready to go!'

The children felt sure he would be ready to go early that night because he had spent so much time out in the storm the night before! Julian and Dick were tired too, but they were quite determined to go up to the shepherd's hill and find the place where they could watch and see if that light really did flash out!

They had a high tea as usual, at which Mr Penruthlan was present. He ate solidly and solemnly, not saying a word except something that sounded like 'Ooahah, ooh.'

'Well, I'm glad you like the pie, Mr Penruthlan,' said his wife. 'Though I say it myself, it's a good one.'

It really was wonderful the way she understood her husband's speech. It was also very strange to hear her speak to her husband as if he was someone to whom she had to be polite, and call Mister! Anne wondered if she called him Mr Penruthlan when they were alone together. She looked at him earnestly. What a dark giant he was – and how he ate!

He looked up and saw Anne watching him. He nodded at her and said 'Ah! Oooh, ock, ukker.' It might have been a foreign language for all Anne could understand! She looked startled and didn't know what to say.

'Now, Mr Penruthlan, don't you tease the child!' said his wife. 'She doesn't know what to answer. Do you, Anne?'

'Well – I – er – I didn't really catch what he said,' said Anne, going scarlet.

'There now, Mr Penruthlan – see how badly you talk without your teeth in!' said the farmer's wife scoldingly. 'Haven't I told you you should wear your teeth when you want to make conversation! I understand you all right, but others don't. It must sound just a mumble to them!'

Mr Penruthlan frowned and muttered something. The children all stared at him, dumbfounded to hear that he had no teeth. Goodness gracious – HOW did he manage to eat all he did, then? He seemed to chew and munch and crunch, and yet he had no teeth!

'So that's why he speaks so oddly,' thought Dick, amused. 'But fancy eating as much as he does, with no teeth in his head! Goodness, what would he eat if he had got all his teeth?'

Mrs Penruthlan changed the conversation because it was clear that her husband was annoyed with her. She talked brightly about the Barnies.

'That horse Clopper! You wait till you see him prance on to the stage, and fall off it. You'll see Mr Penruthlan almost fall out of his seat he laughs so much. He loves that horse. He's seen it a dozen times, and it tickles him to death.'

'I think it's jolly funny myself,' said Julian. 'I've always thought I'd like to put on an act like that at our end-of-term concert at school. Dick and I could do it all right. I wish Sid and Mr Binks would let us try.'

The meal was finished at last. Most of the dishes were empty, and Mrs Penruthlan looked pleased. 'There now – you've done really well,' she said. 'That's what I do like to see, people finishing up everything put before them.'

'It's easy when it's food you put before us,' said George. 'Isn't it, Timmy? I bet Timmy wishes he lived here always, Mrs Penruthlan! I'm sure he keeps telling your dogs how lucky they are!'

from **FIVE GO DOWN TO THE SEA**

A PICNIC ON THE BEACH

THE FIVE were on the beach in two minutes, and Julian undid the basket. It was full of neatly packed sandwiches, and packets of biscuits and chocolate. A bag contained ripe plums, and there were two bottles of lemonade.

'Home-made!' said Dick, taking it out. 'And icy-cold. And what's this? A fruit cake – a whole fruit cake – we're in luck.'

'Woof,' said Timmy, approvingly, and sniffed inside the basket.

Wrapped in brown paper were some biscuits and a bone, together with a small pot of paste. George undid the packet. 'I packed these for you, Timmy,' she said. 'Say thank you!'

Timmy licked her so lavishly that she cried out for mercy. 'Pass me the towel, Ju!' she said. 'Timmy's made my face all wet. Get away now, Timmy – you've thanked me quite enough! Get away, I said. How can I spread paste on your biscuits if you stick your nose into the pot all the time?'

'You spoil Timmy dreadfully,' said Anne. 'All right, all right – you needn't scowl at me, George! I agree that he's worth spoiling. Take your bone a bit farther away from me, Tim – it's smelly!'

They were soon eating sardine sandwiches with tomatoes, and egg-and-lettuce sandwiches after that. Then they started on the fruit cake and the lemonade.

'I can't think why people ever have table-meals when they can have picnics,' said Dick.

from **FIVE HAVE PLENTY OF FUN**

EASTER HOLIDAYS

'The nicest word in the English language is "holidays"!' said Dick, helping himself to a large spoonful of marmalade. 'Pass the toast, Anne. Mother, do you feel downhearted to have us all tearing about the place again?'

'Of course not,' said his mother. 'The only thing that really worries me when holidays come is Food – Food with a capital F. We never seem to have enough in the house when all three of you are back. And by the way – does anyone know what has happened to the sausages that were in the larder?'

'Sausages – sausages – let me think!' said Julian, frowning. Anne gave a sudden giggle. She knew quite well what had happened.

'Well, Mother – you said we could get our own meal last night, as you were out,' said Julian. 'So we poked about and decided on sausages.'

'Yes, but, Julian – two whole packets of sausages!' said his mother. 'I know Georgina came over to spend the evening – but even so . . . !'

'She brought Timmy,' said Anne. 'He rather likes sausages too, Mother.'

'Well, that's the last time I leave the larder door unlocked when I go out!' said her mother. 'Fancy cooking those lovely pork sausages for a dog – especially Timmy, with his enormous appetite! Really, Anne! I meant to have them for our lunch today.'

'Well – we rather thought we'd go and spend the day at Kirrin, with George and Timmy,' said Dick. 'That's if you don't want us for anything, Mother.'

'I do want you,' said his mother. 'Mrs Layman is coming to tea, and she said she wants to see you about something.'

The three groaned, and Dick protested at once. 'Oh, Mother – the first day of the holidays – and we have to be in for tea! It's too bad – a glorious spring day like this, too!'

'Oh – we'll be in for tea all right,' said Julian, giving Dick a sharp little kick

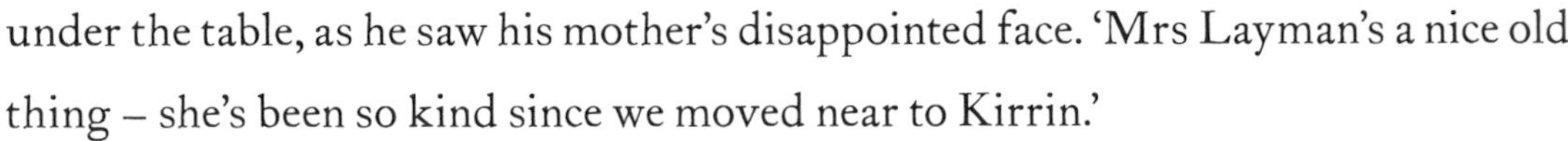

under the table, as he saw his mother's disappointed face. 'Mrs Layman's a nice old thing – she's been so kind since we moved near to Kirrin.'

'And she gave me a present last birthday,' said Anne. 'Do you think we could ask George over too – with Timmy? George will be awfully disappointed if we aren't with her the first day of the hols.'

'Yes, of course you can,' said her mother. 'Go and ring her up now, and arrange it. And don't forget to put our old Tibby-cat in the shed, with a saucer of milk. She's scared stiff of Timmy – he's so enormous. And please, all of you, try to look clean at tea-time.'

'I'll see to Dick and Anne,' said Julian, with a grin. 'I must remember to find their overalls!'

'I'm going to phone George now, this very minute,' said Anne, getting up from the table. 'Do you mind, Mother? I've finished – and I'd like to catch George before she takes Tim for a walk, or does some shopping for Aunt Fanny.'

'Uncle Quentin will be glad to be rid of George, even for a meal,' said Dick. 'He fell over her lacrosse stick yesterday, and wanted to know why she left her fishing net about! George didn't know what he was talking about!'

'Poor old Georgina,' said his mother. 'It's a pity that both she and her father have exactly the same hot tempers. Her mother must find it difficult to keep the peace! Ah – here's Anne back again. Did you get George on the phone, dear?'

'Yes. She's thrilled,' said Anne. 'She says it's just as well we're not going to spend the day with her, because Uncle Quentin has lost some papers he was working on, and he's turning the house upside-down. George said she will probably be mad as a hatter by the time she arrives this afternoon! Uncle Quentin even made Aunt Fanny turn out her knitting bag to see if the papers were there!'

'Dear old Quentin,' said her mother. 'Such a truly brilliant scientist – remembers every book he's ever read – every paper he's ever written – and has the finest brain I know – and yet loses some valuable paper or other almost every week!'

'He loses something else every day of the week too,' said Dick, with a grin. 'His temper! Poor old George – she's always in some sort of trouble!'

'Well, anyway, she's jolly glad to be coming over here!' said Anne. 'She's biking over, with Timmy. She'll be here for lunch. Is that all right, Mother?'

'Of course!' said her mother. 'Now – seeing that you had today's dinner for last night's supper, you'd better do a little shopping for me. What shall we have?'

'SAUSAGES!' said everyone, at once.

'I should have thought you were quite literally fed up with sausages, after last night's feast,' said their mother, laughing. 'All right – sausages. But Timmy can have a bone – a nice meaty bone. I am NOT going to buy any more sausages for him, that's quite certain.'

'And shall we get some nice cakes for tea as Mrs Layman is coming?' said Anne. 'Or are you going to make some, Mother?'

'I'll make a few buns,' said her mother. 'And you can choose whatever else you like – so long as you don't buy up the shop!'

The three went off shopping, cycling along the lane to the village. It was truly a lovely spring day. The celandines were golden in the ditches, and daisies were scattered everywhere. Dick burst into song as they went, and the cows in the nearby fields lifted their heads in surprise as Dick's loud voice swept round them.

Anne laughed. It was good to be with her brothers again. She missed them very much when she was at school. And now they would have almost a whole month together with their cousin George too. She was suddenly overwhelmed with joy, and lifted up her voice and joined Dick in his singing. Her brothers looked at her with affection and amusement.

'Good old Anne,' said Dick. 'You're such a quiet little mouse, it's nice to hear you singing so loudly.'

'I am NOT a quiet little mouse!' said Anne, surprised and rather hurt.

'Whatever makes you say that? You just wait – you may get a surprise one day!'

'Yes – we may!' said Julian. 'But I doubt it. A mouse can't suddenly turn into a tiger! Anyway, one tiger's enough. George is the tiger of our family – my word, she can put out her claws all right – and roar – and rant and rave!'

Everyone laughed at the picture of George as a tiger. Dick wobbled as he laughed and his front wheel touched Anne's back wheel. She turned round fiercely.

'LOOK OUT, IDIOT! You nearly had me over! Can't you see where you're going? Be sensible, can't you?'

'Hey, Anne – whatever's the matter?' said Julian, amazed to hear his gentle little sister lashing out so suddenly.

Anne laughed. 'It's all right. I was just being a tiger for a moment – putting out my claws! I thought Dick and you might like to see them!'

'Well, well!' said Dick, riding beside her. 'I've never heard you yell like that before. Surprising – but quite pleasing! What about you showing old George your claws sometime when she gets out of hand?'

'Stop teasing,' said Anne. 'Here's the butcher's. For goodness sake go and get the sausages, and be sensible. I'll go and buy the cakes.'

The baker's shop was full of new-made buns and cakes, and smelt deliciously of home-made bread. Anne enjoyed herself choosing a vast selection. 'After all,' she thought, 'there will be eight of us – counting Timmy – and if we're all hungry, cakes soon disappear.'

The boys were very pleased to see all the paper bags.

'Looks like a good tea today,' said Dick. 'I hope the old lady – what's her name now? – Layman – who's coming to tea today, has a good appetite. I wonder what she's going to tell us about.'

'Did you buy a nice meaty bone for Timmy?' asked Anne. 'He'll like that for his tea.'

'We bought such a beauty that I'm pretty sure Mother will say it's good enough to make soup from,' said Dick, with a grin. 'So I'll keep it in my saddle-bag till he comes. Dear old Tim. He deserves a jolly good bone. Best dog I ever knew!'

'He's been on a lot of adventures with us,' said Anne, bicycling beside the boys, as the road was empty. 'And he seemed to enjoy them all.'

'Yes. So did we!' said Dick. 'Well – who knows? An adventure may be lying in wait for us these hols too! I seem to smell one in the air!'

from **FIVE HAVE A MYSTERY TO SOLVE**

HOW TO MAKE GINGER BEER

Would you like to make your own delicious fizzy ginger pop to drink at picnics? It's the Famous Five's all-time favourite drink.

Note: this will take several days before it's ready.

Makes 2.5 litres

Ingredients

- fresh ginger (about 15g), unpeeled and finely chopped
- 1 unwaxed lemon, thickly sliced
- 300g golden caster sugar
- ½ tsp cream of tartar
- ¾ tsp dried fast-action yeast
- lemon or lime wedges, to serve

You will also need empty bottles to store 3 litres of liquid. Used mineral water bottles are the easiest, as you don't have to sterilise them – just keep the lids on once they're empty and rinse just before using. For other bottles, run them through the dishwasher and screw their lids back on as soon as they come out.

Method

1. Put all of the ingredients except the yeast into a large pan over a medium heat, along with 750ml of cold water.
2. Slowly bring to the boil, stirring all the time until all the sugar is dissolved, then reduce the heat and simmer for 5 minutes.
3. Turn the heat off, add 1 litre of cold water, sprinkle the yeast on top, cover with a lid and put in a cool place overnight.
4. The next day, strain the entire contents of the pan through a sieve into a big bowl. Then pour the liquid into bottles, leaving a good gap of at least 5cm at the top to allow for the build-up of gas that comes during the fermentation process. This is what makes our ginger beer fizzy!
5. Screw the lids on tightly and put back in the cool place for a second night.
6. The next morning, carefully unscrew the lids and listen for a hiss to check if there has been any build-up of gas. Don't worry if nothing has happened yet. Depending on the yeast, time of year and temperature, it'll probably take 3-5 days to get fizzy, but just in case, check it every 24 hours.
7. When you hear that satisfying fizz as you unscrew the lid, you can move the bottles into the fridge ready to enjoy the ginger beer. Drink within 3 to 4 days.

GET TO KNOW JULIAN

Julian is tall and good-looking with a determined face and brown eyes. He is the oldest of the Five (twelve years old when we first meet him) and he sees himself as the leader.

Julian is good at finding his way around, reading a map and using a compass. Sometimes he can be over-protective – in *Five Go Off in a Caravan*, he suggests locking Anne and George in their caravan at night for their safety. (George replies that Timmy is far better protection than any lock!)

Julian gets on well with most adults. He is helpful and caring to those in need but keen to help the police track down villains. He has a quick tongue and can offer sharp words to nasty adults who try to cross him.

Other people say

It was really impossible to sulk with good-tempered Julian.

I'd bank on Julian to keep the others in order and see they were all safe and sound.

Julian says

You know – I've got a sort of plan coming into my head. Wait a bit – don't interrupt me. I'm thinking.

PETS and THE FAMOUS FIVE

FIVE HAVE A PUZZLING TIME

It was dark and very quiet in Kirrin Cottage – almost midnight.

'Poor George,' said Anne. 'Good thing you're going to the dentist tomorrow!'

'Don't remind me of that!' said George, walking up and down the bedroom. 'Go to sleep, Anne – I didn't mean to disturb you.'

George went to the window and looked out over Kirrin Bay. Timmy jumped off the bed and stood beside her, paws on the windowsill. Suddenly George stiffened and frowned. She stared across the bay, and then turned and called urgently to Anne.

'Anne! Quick, wake up! Come and see! There's a light shining out on Kirrin Island! Somebody's there – on MY island!'

Anne sat up sleepily. 'What's the matter, George? What did you say?'

'I said, there's a light on Kirrin Island! Somebody must be there – without permission too! I'll get my boat and row out right now!'

George was very angry indeed, and Timmy gave a little growl. He would most certainly deal with whoever it was on the island!

George went quickly down to where Dick and Julian lay asleep and shook them roughly. 'Wake up! Something's going on over at Kirrin Island. WAKE UP, Julian.'

George's excited voice not only woke up the boys, but her father as well. Everybody met in the boys' room. 'What on earth is all this about?' demanded George's father.

'There's a light on Kirrin Island,' said George. 'I'm going to see who it is – and so is Timmy. If no one will come with me I'll go alone.'

'Indeed you won't go,' said her father, raising his voice angrily. 'Get back to bed! You can go over tomorrow.'

'I can't!' George almost wailed. 'I've got to go to the dentist. I must go tonight!'

'Shut up, George,' said Julian. 'Be sensible. Whoever's there will still be there tomorrow. Anyway, there's no light there now – you probably made a mistake.'

* * *

'Poor George,' said Anne, as the car went off down the road. 'She does get so worked up about things.'

'Well, anyone gets upset with toothache,' said Julian.

He stared out over Kirrin Bay, which was as blue as cornflowers that morning. 'I wonder if George did see a light on the island last night? You didn't see one, did you, Anne?'

'No. It was all dark there,' said Anne. 'Honestly, I think George must have dreamt it! Anyway she can take out her boat this afternoon, and we'll go with her, and have a good look round!'

'I tell you what,' said Dick, 'we three will get the boat and go over to the island this morning – then, when we find nothing and nobody there – except the rabbits and the jackdaws – we can tell George, and she won't worry any more!'

'Right!' said Julian. 'Let's go now, straight away! Uncle Quentin will be glad to be rid of us – he's working hard this morning on one of his newest problems.'

They went to the beach, to get George's boat. There it was, ready waiting! Julian looked across to where Kirrin Island lay peacefully in the sun. He was quite certain there was nobody there!

'We'll row right round the island and see if there's a boat tied up anywhere, or beached,' said Dick, taking the oars. 'If there isn't, we'll know there's no one there. It's too far for anyone to swim to. Well – here we go!'

Dick rowed the boat carefully between the rocks that guarded the island. 'We'll land at our usual little cove,' he said. 'I'll bet no one else would know how to get there if they didn't already know the way!'

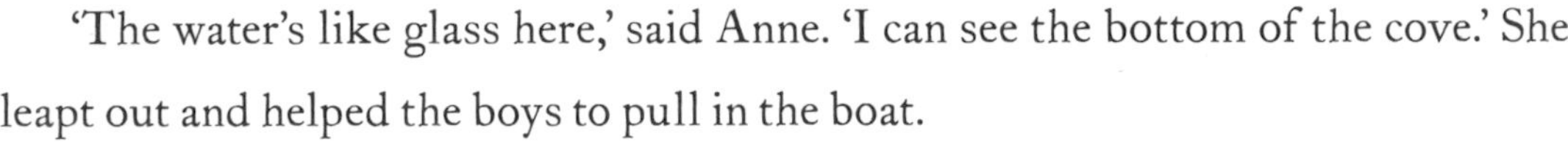

'The water's like glass here,' said Anne. 'I can see the bottom of the cove.' She leapt out and helped the boys to pull in the boat.

They came to the old ruined castle that had been built long ago on the island. Now the jackdaws came down from the tower, and chacked loudly round them in a very friendly manner.

'Well – it doesn't look as if anyone's here,' said Julian, staring round and about.

They went in and out of the old castle, examining the floor – but there was no sign of anyone having made a fire. No matter how they searched, the three could find nothing to explain the light that George had said she saw.

Anne sat down and undid her sandals. She set them by a big stone, so that she could easily find them again, and ran down to the sea.

Soon Julian and Dick came back together, having gone all round the island, and looked into every cranny. They called to Anne.

'We haven't seen a sign of a single soul,' said Dick. 'Better go home again. George may be back by now.'

'I'll put on my sandals,' said Anne, drying her feet in the warm sand. She ran to the big stone by which she had put them. She stopped – and stared in surprise. 'What's happened to one of my sandals? Dick – Ju – have you taken one?'

'Sandals? No – we didn't even know where you'd put them,' said Julian. 'There's one of them there, look – the other must be somewhere near.'

But it wasn't.

'Well! How silly!' said Anne, amazed. 'I know I put them both together, just here. Anyway, why take one, and not both?'

'Perhaps a rabbit took one?' suggested Dick, with a grin. 'Or a jackdaw – they're really mischievous birds, you know!'

'A jackdaw surely couldn't pick up a sandal!' said Anne. 'It'd be too heavy. And I can't imagine a rabbit running off with one!'

'Well – it's not there,' said Dick, thinking that Anne must have been mistaken about putting them both by the big stone. He hunted round, but could not see the other one anywhere – strange!

They were soon all in the boat again, and the boys took it in turn to row back. Through the crowd of rocks they went, threading their way carefully, and at last came to their own beach.

George was there, waiting for them, Timmy beside her!

'You went without me!' she scolded. 'You really are horrible! What did you find?'

'Nothing and no one. The island's absolutely empty except for rabbits and jackdaws!' said Julian, dragging the boat up the sand.

'How's the tooth, George?' said Anne, seeing that George's cheek was still swollen.

But George didn't want to talk about her tooth. 'It's out,' she said, shortly. 'If I hadn't had to go to the dentist, I could have gone with you – and I BET Timmy and I would have found something.'

'All right – go there, then – and take Tim with you,' said Dick, exasperated.

'That's just what I will do!' said George with a scowl. 'We'll soon find out who's hiding there. You can come, too, if you like, of course – but I can't see that you'll be much use!'

'Oh, we'll come all right!' said Dick. 'Even if it's only to say, "Told you so" when you can't find more than we did!'

George had made up her mind to go off in her boat after she had had her dinner.

It wasn't a very happy meal. Even Joanna the cook added a few cross words as she cleared away. 'I'd like to know who's been at the grapes and the oranges,' she said. 'Someone came downstairs in the night and helped themselves. And George – what did you do with the bag of dog biscuits? I couldn't find any for Tim's dinner.'

'Oh don't fuss, Joanna!' said George. 'You know where I always put them – in

the outhouse, with the chicken food.'

'Well, you didn't this time,' said Joanna, huffily.

'I'd like to know something now,' said George. 'Who's been at my big box of chocolates?' She had opened a large box, and was staring inside. 'There's more than half gone!'

But she took herself in hand, helped Joanna with the washing up, and then went to look for the biscuits for Timmy. Sure enough, they were missing, as Joanna had said.

* * *

They soon came to the island. George circled it deftly in the boat, being anxious herself to see that no one had hidden another boat anywhere. She pointed to where a great mass of brown seaweed had piled up on the west shore.

'See what the wind did when we had that terrific gale on Tuesday – brought in masses of seaweed again! Hey – what's wrong with the jackdaws, all of a sudden? Why are they flying up in such a hurry? There is someone on the island!'

George swung the boat round and ran it deftly into the little cove. Out they all leapt, and pulled in the boat. Timmy tore up the beach at full speed, barking.

'That'll scare the life out of anyone hiding!' said George, pleased. 'Go on, Tim – bark. Hunt around! Sniff everywhere!'

They came to a group of bushes and Timmy began to sniff about at once.

'He can smell something there!' said George, excited. 'What is it, Tim?'

But apparently he found nothing of interest, and soon joined them again. Then Anne's sharp eyes caught sight of something bright under a bush. 'Look – orange peel! Someone must have been here then! We'd never leave orange peel about! And look, what's this?'

They all clustered round and looked where Anne was pointing. George bent

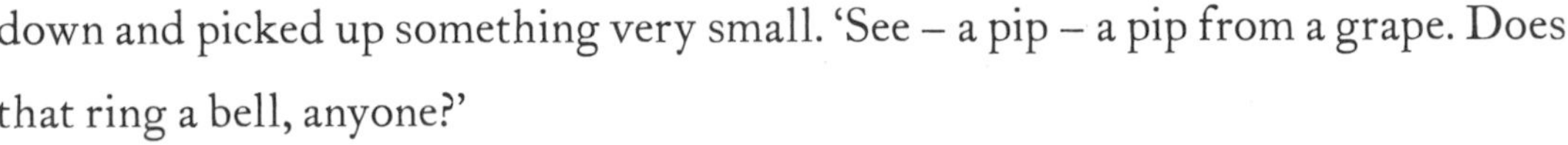

down and picked up something very small. 'See – a pip – a pip from a grape. Does that ring a bell, anyone?'

'Yes!' said Dick. 'Joanna said we'd been at the oranges and grapes – do you think that . . .'

'No! Who's going to steal a bit of fruit and take it over to the island to eat!' said Julian. 'That's too far-fetched, honestly! Let's be sensible!'

'What's Timmy doing?' said Anne, suddenly.

Timmy was feverishly scraping at the sand nearby with his front paws. He gave an excited little bark, that sounded pleased. What on earth had he found? The others ran to him at once.

Timmy had made a hole – and in it something showed. Timmy took hold of it with his teeth, and pulled. It split at once – and to everyone's enormous astonishment, out came a mass of dog biscuits!

Surely, surely they couldn't be the biscuits that George had bought for Timmy the day before, and put in the outhouse?

'They are!' said George. 'Look – exactly the same kind. Who on earth would want to steal dog biscuits and bring them here – and oranges and grapes – and for goodness sake, WHY?'

'Well, that settles it,' said Julian. 'You were right, George – someone is here. But how did they get here without a boat?'

'We'll soon find out!' said George grimly. 'We know he's a thief, anyway! Tim! Find him, find him, whoever he is! Smell him out, Tim!'

Over the sand and on to the rocks went Timmy, right up to where the seaweed was piled in great masses by the wind and the waves. He stopped and began to sniff anxiously.

'He's lost the trail!' said George, disappointed. 'It's the smell of the seaweed that's put him off.'

'Or else whoever was here came in a boat at high tide, which would bring it to the shore – and has sailed off again now the tide has gone out,' said Julian, frowning. 'There wouldn't be any trail to smell, then.'

'Timmy – sniff round again,' said George. 'Go on – you may pick up some other trail.'

Timmy obediently sniffed here and there, and occasionally gave a strange growl of anger. Why? George was puzzled.

George wanted to go on hunting, but the others felt that it was no use. If Timmy had found the scent, and couldn't follow it, no one else would be able to! Anyway, probably the trespasser was far away by now, safely in his boat!

They went back to where they had left their biscuits and bars of chocolate. Anne stopped suddenly and stared down in amazement. 'Look! Half the biscuits have gone – and two of the chocolate bars! Surely the jackdaws couldn't have taken them so quickly!'

'There's a broken biscuit over here. Look – it must have been dropped!' said Dick, amazed. 'I didn't hear a thing!'

'Nor did Tim – or he would have barked,' said George, really puzzled. 'Whoever it was must have come up as quietly as a mouse!'

'Let Timmy sniff round – he'll pick up the trail,' said Julian. 'It'll be so fresh!'

Timmy ran a little way, nose to ground – and then stopped, as if the trail had come to an end!

'Look, Timmy – trails don't finish all of a sudden!' said George, exasperated. 'People don't take off in mid-air!'

'Well, let's hunt round a bit again,' said Julian. 'I know – we'll leave some biscuits and the barley sugars here, and hide – and maybe the thief will come along and take those. He seems to have a sweet tooth!'

'Good idea,' said Dick. 'Come on, everyone – you too, Timmy – and not a sound from anyone, mind!'

They went behind the gorse bush and waited. Dick peeped out once or twice,

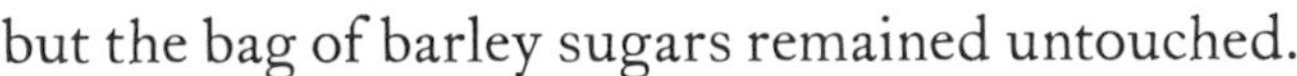

but the bag of barley sugars remained untouched.

Then suddenly Timmy gave a low growl, leapt out and ran at something! Everyone followed in excitement. Who was it?

There was nobody there!

But up on one of the branches of the nearby tree sat the thief, a barley sugar clutched in his hand, chattering angrily.

'It's a monkey – a little monkey!' cried George, in the greatest astonishment. 'It was he who took the other things! Wherever did he come from?'

'Of course!' said Julian. 'This is a puzzle! What do we do next?'

'Well, there's one thing we do know – and that is that a monkey wouldn't light a fire or a lamp at night on the island,' said Dick. 'That must have been done by a human being – and he MUST still be on the island if his monkey's here.'

'Follow the trail again, Tim,' said Julian. 'You may do better this time. Go on!'

But before Timmy could put his head down again, something odd happened. A strange noise came from the west side of the island – the miserable howling of a dog!

'Oh, quick – he sounds as if he's in trouble!' cried George. 'What's happening? Quick, Julian, quick, Timmy! Oh, poor thing, there he goes, howling again. We must find him, we must!'

The Five set off in the direction of the howls, Timmy racing ahead anxiously. He knew far better than the others that a dog was in sore trouble – a howling of that kind meant not only pain, but terror.

Julian was now in front of the other three, and was heading for the seaweed-spread shore on the west of the island. George suddenly gave a cry, and pointed.

'There's the monkey again! He's seen us – he's racing away!'

'Maybe he'll lead us to wherever the dog is,' shouted Julian.

The monkey scampered in front, just ahead of Timmy. They all came to the shore, and stopped when they came to the piled-up heaps of seaweed.

They watched the tiny brown monkey. He was making his way over the seaweed-covered rocks now, avoiding the pools of water here and there. Further and further out he went. George started to go, too, but Julian pulled her back.

'No. That seaweed is slippery – it's too dangerous to go out on those rocks – we know the sea is very deep in between. Look at that little monkey – where on earth does he think he's going?'

The monkey came to a rock that was absolutely covered with thick masses of seaweed flung there by the surging, wind-blown tide. He had no sooner arrived there than an extraordinary thing happened!

A small mass of seaweed moved – and out of it came something that made the Five stare in utter disbelief.

'It can't be!' muttered Dick. 'No – it can't be!'

It was the brown and white head of a big dog! The head suddenly opened a great mouth and howled!

And then another surprising thing happened! A second head poked up from under a covering of seaweed, and a voice shouted loudly, 'Tell your dog to keep off! Mine will fight him! And go away, ALL of YOU!'

* * *

The second head was still poking out of its strange seaweedy hiding place.

'Hey!' yelled Julian. 'We won't hurt you. If you want help, we'll give it to you. Come on out, and tell us what you're doing!'

'All right. But if you try to catch me, I'll set my dog on you!' yelled back a defiant voice. 'He's a cross-bred Alsatian and he could eat up your dog in one gulp!'

And then the seaweed pile was heaved up and down, and out came a scraggy, wet boy. He pulled the seaweed off the dog. The great animal shook itself, and gave one more miserable howl.

The Five were almost too astonished to say a word. The boy looked half scared.

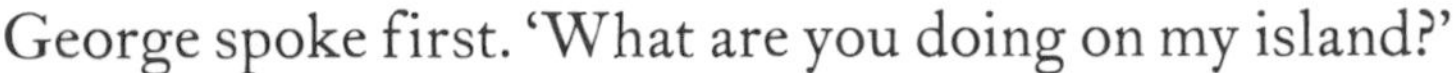

George spoke first. 'What are you doing on my island?'

'My name's Bobby Loman. I live with my Granpop in Kirrin Village. My mum and dad are dead, and I'm on my own – except for Chippy the monkey here, and Chummy, my Alsatian. I've run away. That's all.'

'No,' said Anne gently. 'That isn't all. Tell us everything, Bobby.'

'Oh, well – it's not much,' said Bobby. 'Granpop hates Chippy, because he steals things. And Chummy costs a lot to keep – and – and – you see, he bit someone last week – and Granpop said he was to be put to sleep.' Bobby began to cry, and the Alsatian nestled close to him and licked his cheek. 'He loves me! He's the only person who does.'

George put her arms round Timmy.

'I'm GLAD you came to my island,' said George. 'You and Chippy and Chummy can live here as long as you like. We'll bring you food each day, we'll . . .'

'Hold on, George,' said Julian. 'Don't make promises we can't keep. Let's go back to Kirrin Cottage and tell your mum about this – she'll know what's best to do.'

'Oh – what fun to have another dog and a monkey, as well as Timmy,' said Anne. 'Bobby – how did you come to the island, if you didn't have a boat?'

'Oh – that was easy,' said Bobby. 'I've got one of those blow-up beds. Chippy and I sailed on it, with a spade for an oar – and Chummy swam alongside. It's buried in the sand, so that nobody would see it. But I didn't have any food, so . . .'

'So you crept into our outhouse last night and took a bag of dog biscuits for Chummy, and some fruit for Chippy,' said Julian. 'What about yourself?'

'Oh – I've been eating the dog biscuits,' said Bobby. 'I took some chocolate too. I'm sorry about the stealing. I was desperate, you know.'

'Come on – let's get back home,' said Julian, seeing that Bobby was tired out, cold, wet, and probably very hungry.'

Bobby looked doubtful, but said no more. He cuddled up to Timmy and

Chummy, who both took turns at licking him. Chippy the monkey was very lively and leapt from one person to another, making a funny little chattering noise. He took Dick's handkerchief out of his pocket and pretended to blow his nose on it.

'Hey – you're not to take things from people, I've told you that before!' said Bobby. 'Ooooh – that reminds me – he brought this shoe to me this morning – does it belong to any of you?' And out of his pocket he took – one red sandal!

Anne gave a delighted yell. 'OH! It's mine. I missed it this morning. Oh good – now I won't have to buy a new pair! Chippy – you really are a monkey!'

* * *

George's mother was very astonished to see a monkey, a dog and another boy added to the Five when they arrived at Kirrin Cottage.

'Who are all these?' she said. 'I don't mind the dog, George, but I will not have a monkey running loose in the house.'

'He can sleep in the shed, Mum,' said George. 'Mum, this is Bobby – he ran away from his grandfather.'

'Bobby? Bobby Loman do you mean?' said Mrs Kirrin. 'He was in the papers today. Bobby, your grandfather is very unhappy and worried. I'm sure he would never have had your dog destroyed. He only said that in the heat of the moment – when he was very cross!'

Bobby looked rather scared at Mrs Kirrin's forthright words. George put her arm around his shoulder.

'Mum!' she said, 'I'm sure I'd run away if you threatened to do anything to Timmy – so I do understand why Bobby ran away to my island. Well – sailed away!'

Things were soon settled. Mrs Kirrin rang up the police to tell them Bobby

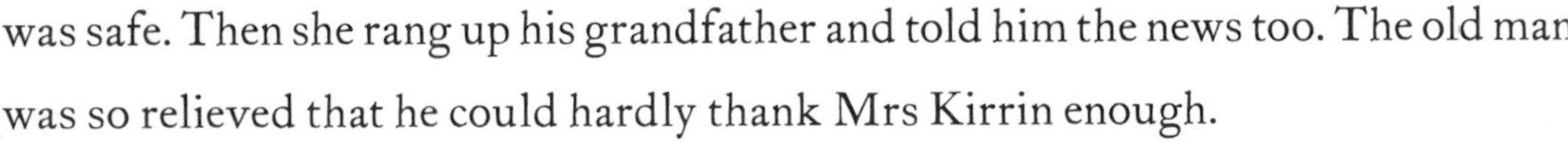

was safe. Then she rang up his grandfather and told him the news too. The old man was so relieved that he could hardly thank Mrs Kirrin enough.

Bobby was allowed to stay the night, and slept in the kitchen on a sofa, with Chippy cuddled beside him, and Chummy on his feet. Upstairs George was in bed with Timmy on her feet, talking about the excitements of the day.

'How's your tooth?' asked Anne, suddenly remembering the night before, when George had had such bad toothache, and seen a light on Kirrin Island.

'Tooth? What tooth?' said George, surprised. She had forgotten all about it. 'Oh, the one I had out. Doesn't it seem AGES since this morning!' She put her tongue into the space where the tooth had been. 'I think a new one's growing already. I wish I had teeth like Timmy – snowy white – strong – fierce. I'd like to be able to show all my teeth, when I feel really angry!'

Anne laughed. 'Well – you almost manage it now,' she said.

'Hey – what's the matter with Timmy? He's pretty restless tonight. Look – he's gone to the door. He wants to go out.'

'All he wants is to go and have a talk to Chummy,' said George. 'All right, Tim. You can go down to the kitchen and sleep with Chummy if you like.'

Timmy pattered down the stairs as soon as the bedroom door was opened. He scraped at the kitchen door and Bobby got up to open it. He was surprised and pleased to see Timmy, who licked him lavishly, and then went to lie beside the pleased Alsatian.

George took one more look out of the window before she got into bed – and gave a sudden exclamation.

'Anne – I think there's a light on Kirrin Island again. Anne – come and look!'

'Don't be an idiot,' said Anne, sleepily. 'You don't think we're going to start this adventure all over again, do you? It's FINISHED, George, not just beginning. Come back to bed.'

George jumped into bed. 'It was a light,' she said, after a moment or two.

'But only a shooting star! What a pity! I'd have liked another adventure – wouldn't you, Anne?'

But Anne was fast asleep, dreaming of monkeys, red sandals, seaweed, big dogs and orange peel.

THE HIDDEN PIT

The Five are staying with their friend Sooty at Smuggler's Top, and his father, Mr Lenoir, and the butler Block won't allow dogs in the house, so Timmy must be hidden ...

THEY SOON settled down at Smuggler's Top. Once George was satisfied that Timmy was safe and happy, though rather puzzled about everything, she settled down too. The only difficulty was getting Timmy to her room at night. This had to be done in darkness. Block had a most tiresome way of appearing silently and suddenly, and George was terrified of him catching a glimpse of the big dog.

Timmy had a strange sort of life the next few days! While the children were indoors, he had to stay in the narrow secret passage, where he wandered about, puzzled and lonely, pricking his ears for a sound of the whistle that meant he was to come to the cupboard and be let out.

He was fed very well, for Sooty raided the larder every night. Sarah, the cook, was amazed at the way things like soup-bones disappeared. She could not understand it. But Timmy devoured everything that was given to him.

Each morning he was given good exercise by the children. The first morning this had been really very exciting!

George had reminded Sooty of his promise to take Timmy for walks each day. 'He simply must have exercise, or he'll be terribly miserable!' she said. 'But how can we manage it? We can't possibly take him through the house and out of the front door! We'd be certain to walk into your father!'

'I told you I knew a way that came out half-way down the hill, silly,' said Sooty. 'I'll show you. We shall be quite safe once we are down there, because even if we met Block or anyone else that knew us, they wouldn't know it was our dog. They would think it was just a stray we had picked up.'

'Well – show us the way,' said George, impatiently. They were all in Sooty's bedroom, and Timmy was lying on the mat beside George. They felt really safe in Sooty's room because of the buzzer that warned them when anyone opened the door at the end of the long passage.

'We'll have to go into Marybelle's room,' said Sooty. 'You'll get a shock when you see the way that leads down the hill, I can tell you!'

He looked out of the door. The door at the end of the passage was shut. 'Marybelle, slip along and peep through the passage door,' said Sooty. 'Warn us if anyone is coming up the stairs. If not, we'll all slip quickly into your room.'

Marybelle ran to the door at the end of the passage. She opened it, and at once the warning buzzer sounded in Sooty's room, making Timmy growl fiercely. Marybelle looked through the doorway to the stair. Then she signalled to the others that no one was coming.

They all rushed out of Sooty's room into Marybelle's, and Marybelle came to join them. She was a funny little mouse of a girl, shy and timid. Anne liked her, and once or twice teased her for being so shy.

But Marybelle did not like being teased. Her eyes filled with tears at once, and she turned away. 'She'll be better when she goes to school,' Sooty said. 'She can't help being shy, shut up all the year round in this strange house. She hardly ever sees anyone of her own age.'

They crowded into the little girl's bedroom and shut the door. Sooty turned the key in the lock. 'Just in case friend Block comes snooping,' he said with a grin.

Sooty began to move the furniture in the room to the sides, near the walls. The others watched in surprise and then helped. 'What's the idea of the furniture removal?' asked Dick, struggling with a heavy chest.

'Got to get this heavy carpet up,' panted Sooty. 'It's put there to hide the trapdoor below. At least, that's what I've always thought.'

Once the furniture stood by the walls, it was easy to drag up the heavy carpet. There was a felt lining under it too, and that had to be pulled aside as well. Then the children saw a trapdoor, let flat into the floor, with a ring-handle to pull it up.

They felt excited. Another secret way! This house seemed full of them. Sooty pulled at the ring and the heavy door came up quite easily. The children peered down, but they could see nothing. It was pitch-dark.

'Are there steps down?' asked Julian, holding Anne back in case she fell.

'No,' said Sooty, reaching out for a big torch he had brought in with him. 'Look!'

He switched on his torch, and the children gave a gasp. The trapdoor led down to a pit, far, far below!

'Why! It's miles below the foundations of the house, surely!' said Julian, surprised. 'It's just a hole down to a big pit. What's it for?'

'Oh, it was probably used to hide people – or to get rid of them!' said Sooty. 'Nice little place, isn't it? If you fell down there you'd land with an awful bump!'

'But – how in the world could we get Timmy down there – or get down ourselves?' said George. 'I'm not going to fall down it, that's certain!'

Sooty laughed. 'You won't have to,' he said. 'Look here.' He opened a cupboard and reached up to a wide shelf. He pulled something down, and the children saw that it was a rope-ladder, fine but very strong.

'There you are! We can all get down by that,' he said.

'Timmy can't,' said George at once. 'He couldn't possibly climb up or down a ladder.'

'Oh, couldn't he?' said Sooty. 'He seems such a clever dog – I should have thought he could easily have done a thing like that.'

'Well, he can't,' said George, decidedly. 'That's a silly idea.'

'I know,' said Marybelle, suddenly, going red at her boldness in breaking in on the conversation. 'I think I know! We could get the laundry basket and shut Timmy in it. And we would tie it with ropes, and let him down – and pull him up the same way!'

The others stared at her. 'Now that really is a brainwave!' said Julian, warmly. 'Good for you, Marybelle. Timmy would be quite safe in a basket. But it would have to be a big one.'

'There's a very big one in the kitchen,' said Marybelle. 'It's never used except when we have lots of people to stay, like now. We could borrow it.'

'Oh yes!' said Sooty. 'Of course we could. I'll go and get it now.'

'But what excuse will you give?' shouted Julian after him. Sooty had already unlocked the door and shot out! He was a most impatient person, and could never put off anything for a single minute.

Sooty didn't answer. He sped down the passage. Julian locked the door after him. He didn't want anyone coming in and seeing the carpet up and the yawning hole!

Sooty was back in two minutes, carrying a very heavy wicker laundry basket on his head. He banged on the door, and Julian unlocked it.

'Good!' said Julian. 'How did you get it? Did anyone mind?'

'Didn't ask them,' grinned Sooty. 'Nobody there to ask. Block's with Father, and Sarah has gone out shopping. I can always put it back if any awkward questions are asked.'

The rope-ladder was shaken out down the hole.

It slipped like an uncoiling snake, down and down, and reached the pit at the bottom. Then Timmy was fetched from Sooty's room. He came in wagging his tail overjoyed at being with everyone again. George hugged him.

'Darling Timmy! I hate you being hidden away like this. But never mind, we're all going out together this morning!'

'I'll go down first,' said Sooty. 'Then you'd better let Timmy down. I'll tie his basket round with this rope. It's nice and strong, and there's plenty to let down. Better tie the other end to the end of the bed, then when we come up again we can easily pull him up.'

Timmy was made to get inside the big basket and lie down. He was surprised and barked a little. But George put her hand over his mouth.

'Sh! You mustn't say a word, Timmy,' she said. 'I know all this is very astonishing. But never mind, you'll have a marvellous walk at the end of it.'

Timmy heard the word 'Walk' and was glad. That was what he wanted – a really nice long walk in the open air and sunshine!

He didn't at all like having the lid shut down on him, but as George seemed to think he must put up with all these strange happenings, Timmy did so, with a very good grace.

'He's really a marvellous dog,' said Marybelle. 'Sooty, get down the hole now, and be ready for when we let him down.'

Sooty disappeared down the dark hole, holding his torch between his teeth. Down and down he went, down and down. At last he stood safely at the bottom, and flashed his torch upwards. His voice came to them, sounding rather strange and far away.

'Come on! Lower Timmy down!'

The laundry basket, feeling extraordinarily heavy now, was pushed to the edge of the hole. Then down it went, knocking against the sides here and there. Timmy growled. He didn't like this game!

Dick and Julian had hold of the rope between them. They lowered Timmy as smoothly as they could. He reached the bottom with a slight bump, and Sooty undid the basket. Out leapt Timmy, barking! But his bark sounded very small and distant to the watchers at the top.

'Now come on down, one by one!' shouted up Sooty, waving his torch. 'Is the door locked, Julian?'

'Yes,' said Julian. 'Look out for Anne. She's coming now.'

Anne climbed down, a little frightened at first, but as her feet grew used to searching for and finding the rungs of the rope-ladder, she went down quite quickly.

Then the others followed, and soon they were all standing together at the bottom of the hole, in the enormous pit. They looked round curiously. It had a musty smell, and its walls were damp and greenish. Sooty swung his torch round, and the children saw various passages leading off here and there.

'Where do they all lead to?' asked Julian, in amazement.

'Well, I told you this hill was full of tunnels,' said Sooty. 'This pit is down in the hill and these tunnels lead into the catacombs. There are miles and miles of them. No one explores them now, because so many people have been lost in them and never heard of again. There used to be an old map of them, but it's lost.'

'It's weird!' said Anne, and shivered. 'I wouldn't like to be down here alone.'

'What a place to hide smuggled goods in,' said Dick. 'No one would ever find them here.'

'I guess the old-time smugglers knew every inch of these passages,' said Sooty. 'Come on! We'll take the one that leads out of the hillside. We'll have to do a bit of climbing when we get there. I hope you don't mind.'

'Not a bit,' said Julian. 'We're all good climbers. But I say, Sooty – you're sure you know the way? We don't want to be lost for ever down here!'

'Course I know the way! Come on!' said Sooty, and, flashing his torch in front of him, he led the way into the dark and narrow tunnel.

from **FIVE GO TO SMUGGLER'S TOP**

THE CIRCUS CAMP AND NOBBY

It did not take the caravans very long to come in sight of the circus camp. As George had said, it was in a comfortable hollow, set at the foot of the hills – a quiet spot, well away from any dwelling-places, where the circus animals could enjoy a certain amount of freedom and be exercised in peace.

The caravans were set round in a wide circle. Tents had been put up here and there. The big elephant was tied by a thick rope to a stout tree. Dogs ran about everywhere, and a string of shining horses was being paraded round a large field nearby.

'There they all are!' said Anne, excitedly, standing up on the driving seat to see better. 'Golly, the chimpanzee is loose, isn't he? No, he isn't – someone has got him on a rope. Is it Nobby with him?'

'Yes, it is. I say, fancy walking about with a live chimp like that!' said Julian.

The children looked at everything with the greatest interest as their caravans came nearer to the circus camp. Few people seemed to be about that hot afternoon. Nobby was there with the chimpanzee, and one or two women were stirring pots over small fires – but that seemed to be all.

The circus dogs set up a great barking as the red and green caravans drew nearer. One or two men came out of the tents and looked up the track that led to the camp. They pointed to the children's caravans and seemed astonished.

Nobby, with the chimpanzee held firmly by the paw, came out of the camp in curiosity to meet the strange caravans. Julian hailed him.

'Hi, Nobby! You didn't think you'd see us here, did you?'

Nobby was amazed to hear his name called. At first he did not remember the children at all. Then he gave a yell.

'Jumping Jiminy, it's you kids I saw away back on the road! What are you doing here?'

Timmy growled ominously and George called to Nobby. 'He's never seen a chimpanzee before. Do you think they'll be friends?'

'Don't know,' said Nobby doubtfully. 'Old Pongo likes the circus dogs all right. Anyway, don't you let your dog fly at Pongo, or he'll be eaten alive! A chimp is very strong, you know.'

'Could I make friends with Pongo, do you think?' asked George. 'If he would shake hands with me, or something, Timmy would know I was friends with him and he'd be all right. Would Pongo make friends with me?'

'Course he will!' said Nobby. 'He's the sweetest-tempered chimp alive – aren't you, Pongo? Now, shake hands with the lady.'

Anne didn't feel at all inclined to go near the chimpanzee, but George was quite fearless. She walked up to the big animal and held out her hand. The chimpanzee took it at once, raised it to his mouth and pretended to nibble it, making friendly noises all the time.

George laughed. 'He's nice, isn't he?' she said. 'Timmy, this is Pongo, a friend. Nice Pongo, good Pongo!'

She patted Pongo on the shoulder to show Timmy that she liked the chimpanzee, and Pongo at once patted her on the shoulder, too, grinning amiably. He then patted her on the head and pulled one of her curls.

Timmy wagged his tail a little. He looked very doubtful indeed. What was this strange creature that his mistress appeared to like so much? He took a step towards Pongo.

'Come on, Timmy, say how do you do to Pongo,' said George. 'Like this.' And she shook hands with the chimpanzee again. This time he wouldn't let her hand go, but went on shaking it up and down as if he was pumping water with a pump handle.

'He won't let go,' said George.

'Don't be naughty, Pongo,' said Nobby in a stern voice. Pongo at once dropped

George's hand and covered his face with a hairy paw as if he was ashamed. But the children saw that he was peeping through his fingers with wicked eyes that twinkled with fun.

'He's a real monkey!' said George, laughing.

'You're wrong – he's an ape!' said Nobby. 'Ah, here comes Timmy to make friends. Jumping Jiminy, they're shaking paws!'

So they were. Timmy, having once made up his mind that Pongo was to be a friend, remembered his manners and held out his right paw as he had been taught. Pongo seized it and shook it vigorously. Then he walked round to the back of Timmy and shook hands with his tail. Timmy didn't know what to make of it all.

The children yelled with laughter, and Timmy sat down firmly on his tail. Then he stood up again, his tail wagging, for Barker and Growler had come rushing up. Timmy remembered them, and they remembered him.

'Well, they're making friends all right,' said Nobby, pleased. 'Now they'll introduce Timmy to all the other dogs, and there'll be no trouble. Hey, look out for Pongo, there!'

The chimpanzee had stolen round to the back of Julian and was slipping his hand into the boy's pocket. Nobby went to him and slapped the chimpanzee's paw hard.

'Naughty! Bad boy! Pickpocket!'

The children laughed again when the chimpanzee covered his face with his paws, pretending to be ashamed.

from **FIVE GO OFF IN A CARAVAN**

A SURPRISING SIGNAL

'Why did you signal eighteen times, Uncle Quentin?' asked Anne.

'Ah, well – it's difficult to explain, really,' said her uncle. 'The fact is – I can't help feeling there's somebody else on this island besides myself!'

'Quentin! What in the world do you mean?' cried Aunt Fanny, in alarm. She looked over her shoulder as if she half expected to see somebody there. All the children stared in amazement at Uncle Quentin.

He took another sandwich. 'Yes, I know it sounds mad. Nobody else could possibly have got here. But I know there is someone!'

'Oh don't, Uncle!' said Anne, with a shiver. 'It sounds horrid. And you're all alone at night too!'

'Ah, that's just it! I wouldn't mind a bit if I was all alone at night!' said her uncle. 'What worries me is that I don't think I shall be all alone.'

'Uncle, what makes you think there's somebody here?' asked Julian.

'Well, when I had finished the experiment I was doing last night – about half past three in the early morning it would be – but pitch-dark, of course,' said Uncle Quentin, 'I came into the open for a breath of fresh air. And I could swear I heard somebody cough – yes, cough twice!'

'Good gracious!' said Aunt Fanny, startled. 'But Quentin – you might have been mistaken. You do imagine things sometimes, you know, when you're tired.'

'Yes, I know,' said her husband. 'But I couldn't imagine this, could I?'

He put his hand into his pocket and took something out. He showed it to the others. It was a cigarette end, quite crisp and fresh.

'Now, I don't smoke cigarettes. Nor do any of you! Well then – who smoked that cigarette? And how did he come here? No one would bring him by boat – and that's the only way here.'

There was a silence. Anne felt scared. George stared at her father, puzzled.

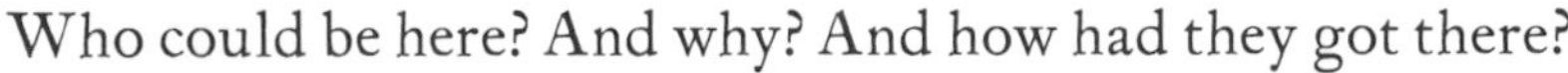

Who could be here? And why? And how had they got there?

'Well, Quentin – what are you going to do?' said his wife. 'What would be best?'

'I'll be all right if George will give her consent to something,' said Uncle Quentin. 'I want Timmy here, George! Will you leave him behind with me?'

There was a horrified silence. George stared at her father in complete dismay. Everyone waited to see what she would say.

'But, Father – Timmy and I have never been separated once,' she said at last, in a pleading voice. 'I do see you want him to guard you – and you can have him – but I'll have to stay here too!'

'Oh no!' said her father at once. 'You can't possibly stay, George. That's out of the question. As for never being separated from Timmy, well, surely you wouldn't mind that for once? If it was to ensure my safety?'

George swallowed hard. This was the most difficult decision she had ever had to make in her life. Leave Timmy behind on the island – where there was some unknown hidden enemy, likely to harm him if he possibly could!

And yet there was Father too – he might be in danger if there was no one to guard him.

'I shall just have to stay here, Father,' she said. 'I can't leave Timmy behind unless I stay too. It's no good.'

Her father began to lose his temper. He was like George – he wanted his own way, and if he didn't have it he was going to make a fuss!

'If I'd asked Julian or Dick or Anne this same thing, and they'd had a dog, they would all have said yes, at once!' he raged. 'But you, George, you must always make things difficult if you can! You and that dog – anyone would think he was worth a thousand pounds!'

'He's worth much more than that to me,' said George, in a trembling voice. Timmy crept nearer to her and pushed his nose into her hand. She held his collar as if she would not let him go for a moment.

'Yes. That dog's worth more to you than your father or mother or anyone,' said her father, in disgust.

'No, Quentin, I can't have you saying things like that,' said his wife, firmly. 'That's just silly. A mother and father are quite different from a dog – they're loved in different ways. But you are perfectly right, of course – Timmy must stay behind with you – and I shall certainly not allow George to stay with him. I'm not going to have both of you exposed to danger. It's bad enough to worry about you, as it is.'

George looked at her mother in dismay.

'Mother! Do tell Father I must stay here with Timmy.'

'Certainly not,' said her mother. 'Now, George, be unselfish. If it were left to Tim to decide, you know perfectly well that he would stay here – and stay without you. He would say to himself, "I'm needed here – my eyes are needed to spy out enemies, my ears to hear a quiet footfall – and maybe my teeth to protect my master. I shall be parted from George for a few days – but she, like me, is big enough to put up with that!" That's what Timmy would say, George, if it were left to him.'

Everyone had been listening to this unexpected speech with great attention. It was about the only one that could persuade George to give in willingly!

She looked at Timmy. He looked back at her, wagging his tail. Then he did an extraordinary thing – he got up, walked over to George's father, and lay down beside him, looking at George as if to say, 'There you are! Now you know what I think is right!'

'You see?' said her mother. 'He agrees with me. You've always said that Timmy was a good dog, and this proves it. He knows what his duty is. You ought to be proud of him.'

'I am,' said George, in a choky voice. She got up and walked off. 'All right,' she

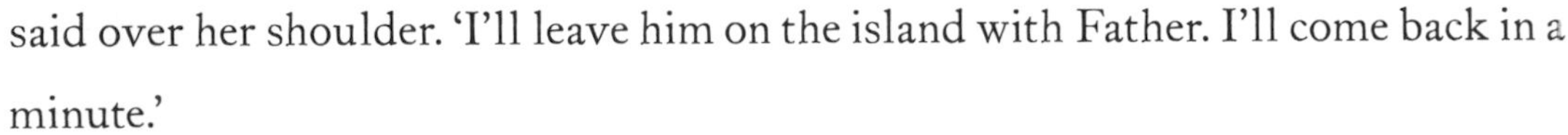

said over her shoulder. 'I'll leave him on the island with Father. I'll come back in a minute.'

Anne got up to go after poor George, but Julian pulled her down again. 'Leave her alone! She'll be all right. Good old Timmy – you know what's right and what's wrong, don't you? Good dog, splendid dog!'

Timmy wagged his tail. He did not attempt to follow George. No – he meant to stay by her father now, even though he would much rather be with his mistress. He was sorry that George was unhappy – but sometimes it was better to do a hard thing and be unhappy about it, than try to be happy without doing it.

'Oh, Quentin dear, I don't like this business of you being here and somebody else spying on you,' said his wife, 'I really don't. How long will it be before you've finished your work?'

'A few days more,' said her husband. He looked at Timmy admiringly. 'That dog might almost have known what you were saying, Fanny, just now. It was remarkable the way he walked straight over to me.'

'He's a very clever dog,' said Anne warmly. 'Aren't you, Tim? You'll be quite safe with him, Uncle Quentin. He's terribly fierce when he wants to be!'

'Yes. I shouldn't care to have him leaping at my throat,' said her uncle. 'He's so big and powerful. Are there any more pieces of cake?'

'Quentin, it's really too bad of you to go without your meals,' said his wife. 'It's no good telling me you haven't, because you wouldn't be as ravenous as this if you had had your food regularly.'

Her husband took no notice of what she was saying.

He was looking up at his tower. 'Do you ever see those wires at the top blaze out?' he asked. 'Wonderful sight, isn't it?'

'Uncle, you're not inventing a new atom bomb, or anything are you?' asked Anne.

Her uncle looked at her scornfully. 'I wouldn't waste my time inventing things that will be used to kill and maim people! No – I'm inventing something that will be of the greatest use to mankind. You wait and see!'

George came back. 'Father,' she said, 'I'm leaving Timmy behind for you – but please will you do something for me?'

'What?' asked her father. 'No silly conditions now! I shall feed Timmy regularly, and look after him, if that's what you want to ask me. I may forget my own meals, but you ought to know me well enough to know I shouldn't neglect any animal dependent on me.'

'Yes – I know, Father,' said George, looking a bit doubtful all the same. 'What I wanted to ask you was this – when you go up in the tower to signal each morning, will you please take Timmy with you? I shall be up at the coastguard's cottage, looking through his telescope at the glass room in the tower – and I shall be able to see Timmy then. If I catch just a glimpse of him each day and know he's all right, I shan't worry so much.'

'Very well,' said her father. 'But I don't suppose for a moment that Timmy will be able to climb up the spiral stairway.'

'Oh, he can, Father – he's been up it once already,' said George.

'Good heavens!' said her father. 'Has the dog been up there too? All right, George – I promise I'll take him up with me each morning that I signal, and get him to wag his tail at you. There! Will that satisfy you?'

'Yes. Thank you,' said George. 'And you'll give him a few kind words and a pat occasionally, Father, won't you . . . and . . . ?'

'And put his bib on for him at mealtimes, I suppose, and clean his teeth for him at night!' said her father, looking cross again. 'I shall treat Timmy like a proper grown-up dog, a friend of mine, George – and believe me, that's the way he wants me to treat him. Isn't it, Timmy? You like all those frills to be kept for your mistress, don't you, not for me?'

'Woof,' said Timmy, and thumped his tail. The children looked at him admiringly. He really was a very sensible, clever dog. He seemed somehow much more grown-up than George.

'Uncle, if anything goes wrong, or you want help or anything, flash eighteen times again,' said Julian. 'You ought to be all right with Timmy. He's better than a dozen policemen – but you never know.'

'Right. Eighteen flashes if I want you over here for anything,' said his uncle. 'I'll remember. Now you'd better all go. It's time I got on with my work.'

'You'll pour that soup away, won't you, Quentin?' said his wife, anxiously. 'You don't want to make yourself ill by eating bad soup. It must be green by now! It would be so like you to forget all about it while it was fresh and good – and only remember when it was bad!'

'What a thing to say!' said her husband, getting up. 'Anyone would think I was five years old, without a brain in my head, the way you talk to me!'

'You've plenty of brains dear, we all know that,' said his wife. 'But you don't seem very old sometimes! Now, look after yourself – and keep Timmy by you all the time.'

'Father won't need to bother about that,' said George. 'Timmy will keep by him! You're on guard, Timmy, aren't you? And you know what that means!'

'Woof,' said Timmy, solemnly. He went with them all to the boat, but he did not attempt to get in. He stood by George's father and watched the boat bob away over the water. 'Goodbye, Timmy!' shouted George, in a funny fierce voice. 'Look after yourself!'

Her father waved, and Timmy wagged his tail. George took one of the pairs of oars from Dick and began to row furiously, her face red with the hard work.

Julian looked at her in amusement. It was hard work for him, too, to keep up with the furious rowing, but he didn't say anything. He knew all this fury in rowing was George's way of hiding her grief at parting with Timmy. Funny old

George! She was always so intense about things – furiously happy or furiously unhappy, in the seventh heaven of delight or down in the very depths of despair or anger.

from **FIVE ON KIRRIN ISLAND AGAIN**

GEORGE GETS A HEADACHE!

Henrietta went up to Julian. 'Look, I guess it's because you've asked me to come, that Georgina won't come with us. I don't want to spoil things. You go and tell her I'm not going after all.'

Julian looked at Henry gratefully. 'That's jolly nice of you,' he said. 'But we're taking George at her word. Anyway, we didn't ask you out of politeness. We wanted you to come!'

'Thanks,' said Henry. 'Well, let's go before anything else happens! Our horses are ready. I'll fix the saddle-bags.'

Soon all four were on their horses, and were walking over the yard to the gate. George heard the clippity-clop-clippity-clop of the hooves and peeped out of the window again. They were going after all! She hadn't thought they really would go without her. She was horrified.

'Why did I behave like that? I've put myself in the wrong!' thought poor George. 'Now Henrietta will be with them all day and will be as nice as possible, just to show me up. What an ass I am!'

'Timmy, I'm an ass and an idiot, and a great big idiot! Aren't I?'

Timmy didn't think so. He had been puzzled to hear the others going off without him and George, and had gone to the door and whined. Now he came back to George and put his head on her knee. He knew George was not happy.

'You don't care how I behave, do you, Tim?' said George, stroking the soft, furry head. 'That's the best thing about a dog! You don't care if I'm in the wrong or not, you just love me all the same, don't you? Well, you shouldn't love me today, Tim. I've been an idiot!'

There was a knock at her door. It was William again. 'George! Mrs Johnson says, if your headache is bad, undress and get into bed. But if it's better, come down and help with Clip, the traveller's horse.'

'I'll come down,' said George, flinging away her sulks at one go. 'Tell Mrs Johnson I'll go to the stable at once.'

'All right,' said the stolid William, and trotted off like a reliable little pony.

George went downstairs with Timmy, and into the yard. She wondered how far the others had gone. She couldn't see them in the distance. Would they have a good day together, with that horrid Henry? Ugh!

The others were almost a mile away, cantering easily. What fun! A whole day before them, on Mystery Moor.

* * *

George had had quite an interesting day. First she had gone down to help Captain Johnson do Clip's leg again and bandage it up. The little skewbald stood very patiently, and George felt a sudden liking for the ugly little creature.

'Thanks, George,' said Captain Johnson, who, to her relief, had said nothing about her not having gone riding with the others. 'Now would you like to come and put jumps up for the youngsters? They're longing to do some more jumping.'

George found that it was quite amusing to teach the younger ones how to jump. They were so very, very proud of themselves when they went over even a foot-high jump on their little ponies.

After that Sniffer arrived, accompanied by a peculiar little mongrel called Liz. Liz was a bit of a spaniel, a bit of a poodle, and odd bits of something else – and looked rather like a small, walking hearth rug of black curly fur.

Timmy was amazed to see this walking mat, and sat and watched Liz sniffing here and there for some time, before he came to the conclusion that it really was some kind of dog. He gave a sharp little bark to see what this comical creature would do when she heard it.

Liz took no notice at all. She had unearthed a small bone, which smelt extremely interesting. Timmy considered that all bones within the radius of at least a mile belonged to him and him alone. So he ran over to Liz at once and gave a small, warning growl.

Liz immediately dropped the bone humbly at his feet, then sat up on her hind legs and begged. Timmy eyed her in astonishment. Then Liz stood up on her hind legs and walked daintily all round Timmy and back again.

Timmy was astounded. He had never seen a dog do that before. *Could* this hearth rug affair be a dog after all?

Liz saw that Timmy was really impressed, and went on with yet another trick she had learnt during the time she had been with the circus.

She turned head-over-heels, yapping all the time. Timmy retreated a few steps into the bushes. This was going too far! What was this animal doing? Trying to stand on its head?

Liz went on turning head-over-heels very rapidly and ended up almost on Timmy's front paws. He had now backed into the bush as far as he could.

Liz remained on her back, paws in the air, tongue hanging out, panting. She gave a very small, beseeching whine.

Timmy bent his head down and sniffed at her paws. Behind him his tail began to move a little – yes, it had a wag in it! He sniffed again. Liz leapt on to her four feet and pranced all round Timmy, yapping as if to say, 'Come on and play! Do come!'

And then suddenly Timmy fell upon the absurd little creature and pretended to worry it. Liz gave a delighted volley of yaps and rolled over and over. They had a marvellous game, and when it was all over, Timmy sank down panting for breath in a sunny corner of the yard and Liz settled herself between his front paws, as if she had known him all her life!

When George came out of the stable with Sniffer, she could hardly believe her eyes. 'What's that Timmy's got between his paws?' she said. 'It's surely not a dog!'

'It's Liz,' said Sniffer. 'She can get round any dog there is, George! Liz! You're a monkey, aren't you! Walk, then, walk!'

Liz left Timmy and ran over to Sniffer, walking daintily on her hind legs. George laughed. 'What a funny little creature, like a bit cut out of a furry hearth rug!'

from **FIVE GO TO MYSTERY MOOR**

A FEW UPSETS

Berta, an American girl, has arrived at Kirrin Cottage late one night. The following morning she sits down to breakfast with George, her cousins and her parents, Quentin and Fanny.

'QUENTIN – THAT's the second time this month you've spread your toast with mustard instead of with marmalade,' said his wife. 'Do have a little sense.'

After that everyone became very cheerful. Uncle Quentin laughed at himself, and George saw the funny side and laughed loudly too, which made Timmy bark, and Berta giggled. Aunt Fanny was quite relieved that her husband had done such a silly thing.

'Do you remember when Father poured custard all over his fried fish once?' George said, entering into the talk for the first time. 'And he said it was the best egg sauce he had ever tasted?'

The conversation was very animated after that, and Aunt Fanny felt happier. 'You children can clear away and wash up the breakfast things for Joanna,' she said. 'Or two of you can and the others can make the beds with me.'

'What about my little dog?' said Berta, suddenly remembering her again. 'I haven't seen her yet, because I was only just in time for breakfast. Where is she?'

'You can go and get her now,' said Aunt Fanny. 'We've all finished. Are you going to start your work, Quentin?'

'Yes, I am,' said her husband. 'So I don't want any yelling or shouting or barking outside my study door.'

He got up and went out of the room. Berta stood up too. 'Where's the kennel?' she said.

'I'll show you,' said Anne. 'We'll go and get your dog and introduce it to Timmy. Coming, George?'

'You can bring the dog in here, and we'll see what Timmy says,' said George, going all gloomy again. 'If he doesn't like the dog – and he won't – it will have to live out in the kennel.'

'Oh no,' said Berta, at once.

'Well, you don't want Timmy to eat it, do you?' said George. 'He's very jealous of other dogs in the house. He might go for yours and savage it.'

'Oh no!' said Berta, again, looking upset. 'Timmy's nice. He's not a fierce dog.'

'That's all you know!' said George. 'Well, I've warned you.'

'Come on,' said Anne, pulling at Berta's sleeve. 'Let's go and fetch Sally. She must be wondering why nobody bothers about her. I bet Timmy won't mind terribly.'

As soon as the two had gone out, George spoke in Timmy's ear. 'You don't like strange dogs who want to come and live here, do you, Tim? You'll growl and snarl like anything, won't you? Growl your very fiercest! I know you won't bite but if you could just growl your loudest, that will be enough. Berta will make that Sally-dog live out of doors then!'

Soon she heard footsteps returning, and Anne's voice exclaiming in delight.

'Oh, she's sweet! Oh, what a darling! Sally, you're a pet! Julian, Dick, Aunt Fanny – do come and see Berta's dog!'

Everyone came into the room, led by Berta and Anne. Berta held the dog in her arms.

It was a tiny black poodle, whose woolly fur was cut away here and there to give it a very funny look. Sally was certainly an attractive little thing! Her sharp little nose sniffed all the time she was carried into the room, and her quick little eyes looked everywhere.

Berta put her down, and the little poodle stood there, poised on her dainty feet like a ballet dancer about to perform. Everyone but George exclaimed in delight.

'She's a poppet!'

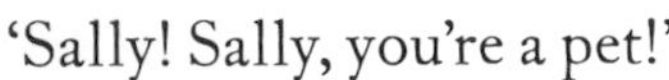

'Sally! Sally, you're a pet!'

'Oh, a poodle! I do love poodles! They look so knowing.'

Timmy stood by George, sniffing hard to get the smell of this new dog. George had her hand on his collar in case he sprang. His tail was as stiff as a ramrod.

The poodle suddenly saw him. She stared at him out of bright little eyes, quite unafraid. Then she pulled away from Berta's hand and trotted right over to Timmy, her funny little tail wagging merrily.

Timmy backed a little in surprise. The poodle danced all round him on her toes, and gave a little whimpering bark, which said as plainly as possible, 'I want to play with you!'

Timmy sprang. He leapt in the air and came down with a thud on his big paws, and the little poodle dodged. Timmy's tail began to wag wildly. He sprang again in play, and almost knocked the little poodle over. He barked as if to say, 'Sorry, I didn't mean that!'

Then he and the poodle played a most ridiculous game of dodge and run, and although one or two chairs went flying, nobody minded – they were all laughing so much at the sight of the quick little poodle leading Timmy such a dance.

At last Sally was tired and sat down in a corner. Timmy pranced about in front of her, showing off. Then he went up to her and sniffed her nose. He licked it gently, and then lay down in front of her, gazing at her adoringly.

Anne gave a little squeal of laughter. 'He's gazing at Sally exactly as he gazes at you, George!' she cried.

But George was not at all pleased. In fact she was quite astounded. To think that Timmy should welcome another dog! To think that he should behave like this when she had told him to do the opposite!

'Aren't they sweet together?' said Berta, pleased. 'I thought Timmy would like Sally. Of course Sally is a pedigree dog, and cost a lot of money – and Timmy's only a mongrel. I expect he thinks she's wunnerful.'

'Oh, Tim may be a mongrel, but he's absolutely wunnerful too,' said Dick, hastily, pronouncing the word like Berta, to try and get a laugh. He saw George's scowl, and knew how cross she felt at hearing her beloved Timmy compared with a pedigree dog. 'He's a magnificent fellow, aren't you, Timmy?' went on Dick. 'Sally may be a darling, but you're worth more than a hundred darlings, aren't you?'

'I think he's beautiful,' said Berta, looking down at Timmy. 'He's got the loveliest eyes I ever did see.'

George began to feel a little better. She called Timmy. 'You're making rather a fool of yourself,' she said to him.

'Now that Timmy and Sally are going to be friends, can I have Sally to sleep on my bed at night, like George has Timmy?' said Berta. 'Please say yes, Aunt Fanny.'

from **FIVE HAVE PLENTY OF FUN**

BILLYCOCK FARM

They were in a big farmyard, with hens pecking around them and ducks swimming on a round duck pond. Farm dogs began barking from somewhere – and then something ran round the corner of the old house - something very small and pink.

'Whatever is it?' said Anne. 'Oh - it's a pigling! What a pet! Oh it's come right up to us – little pigling, have you escaped from your sty? How clean you are!'

The tiny pig gave funny little squeals, and ran up to Timmy, who sat back on his haunches in surprise, staring at this unexpected little creature. He thought it must be some sort of dog without any hair.

The pigling butted Timmy gently and Timmy retreated backwards. Julian laughed. 'Tim can't make it out!' he said. 'No, don't growl, Timmy – it's quite harmless!'

'Hallo – who's this?' said Dick as a small figure came round the house. It stopped when it saw the Five.

'What a dear little boy!' said Anne. 'Is he Toby's brother?'

The child didn't look more than five years old. He had a head of bright yellow curls, big brown eyes, and a grin just like his big brother's.

'That's my pig,' he said, coming slowly towards them. 'He runned away from me.'

Anne laughed. 'What's your pig's name?' she said.

'Curly,' said the small boy, and pointed at the pigling's tail. 'He's got a curly tail. It won't go straight.'

'It's a nice tail,' said Anne. The pigling ran to the small boy, and he grabbed it by its tail. 'You runned away again,' he said. Then he picked up the pig and walked off.

'Hey! Is this Billycock Farm?' called Julian. 'Have you got a brother called Toby?'

'Toby? Yes, Toby's over there,' said the boy, and he pointed to a big barn. 'Toby's ratting with Binky.'

'Right,' said Julian. The little boy disappeared with his funny pet, and Julian laughed. 'He's rather a pet himself,' he said. 'Come on – let's go and find Toby and Binky. Perhaps Binky is another brother.'

'Or a dog,' said George, and put her hand on Timmy's collar. 'Better be careful. He might go for Tim.'

'Yes – Binky might be a dog, of course – probably a good ratter,' said Julian. 'Dick and I will go to the barn and you two girls stay here with Timmy.'

They went off to the barn. A great noise came from inside as the two boys approached. Shouts and barks and the rap of a stick came to their ears.

'Get him, Binky – look, he went under that sack! Oh, you fathead, you've lost him again!'

Wuff-wuff-wuff! Rap-rap! More yells! In great curiosity Julian and Dick peered into the rather dark old barn. They saw Toby there, prodding under sacks, with a most excited collie beside him, barking incessantly.

'Hey, Toby!' yelled Julian, and Toby stood up and turned a red and perspiring face towards the two boys.

'Oh – you've arrived!' he said, going quickly to the door. 'I thought you were never coming. Glad to see you! But are there only two of you? I got out tents and things for four.'

'There are four of us – five counting Timmy,' said Julian. 'We've left the two girls over there with him – he's our dog. Will yours be friendly or not?'

'Oh, yes, so long as I introduce them,' said Toby and they all went out of the barn. As soon as Binky, Toby's dog, saw Timmy, he stood still, made himself stiff and growled, while the hackles on his neck slowly rose up.

'It's all right,' shouted Toby to the girls. 'Bring your dog here. He'll be all right with Binky in half a minute.'

Rather doubtfully George brought Timmy across. Timmy was a bit doubtful himself of this big collie! Toby bent down and spoke into Binky's ear.

'Binky, shake paws with this nice girl – she's a friend.'

He nodded at George. 'Hold out your hand,' he said.

George bent down to the collie and held out her hand. At once the dog put up his paw and allowed her to shake it solemnly.

'Now you,' said Toby to Anne, and she did the same. She liked this dog Binky, with his bright brown eyes and long, sleek nose.

'Does your dog shake hands, too?' asked Toby. George nodded. 'He does? Right – tell him to shake paws with Binky. Binky, shake!'

'Timmy, shake,' commanded George, and very politely and solemnly the two dogs shook paws, eyeing each other cautiously. Timmy gave a sudden little whine – and then the two were tearing round the yard together, barking furiously, chasing one another, rolling over and having a wonderful game.

'That's all right, then,' said Toby, pleased. 'Binky's quite all right with anyone, human or animal, so long as he can shake hands with them. I've taught him that. But he's a dud ratter! He just can't seem to nip a rat. Well – let's go and see my mother. She's expecting you. She's got a whopping great tea.'

This was all very satisfactory! Just the kind of welcome the Five liked. Anne looked sideways at Toby. She thought he was rather nice. George wasn't so sure. He had a rose in his buttonhole – was it a trick one, and was he going to ask her to smell it?

'We saw a little yellow-haired boy just now,' said Anne. 'With a tiny pigling.'

'Oh, that's Benny with his pet pig,' said Toby, laughing. 'He calls it Curly – and he adores it! We've offered him a kitten or a puppy – but no, he wants that pigling. They go everywhere together – like Mary and her lamb! Benny's a pet – he really is. Kid brothers are usually a nuisance, you know, but Benny isn't.'

MISCHIEF, TINKER – AND TIMMY!

'LOOK AT Mischief – he's helping himself to apples in the larder, but you don't say anything to him!'

'Oh, lands sakes, is that creature in the larder again?' cried poor Joanna, rushing across the kitchen. 'Who left it open, I'd like to know?'

'Timmy did,' said Tinker.

'You little liar!' said Joanna as she shooed Mischief out of the larder. 'Timmy would never do a thing like that. He's as honest as the day, not like that little thief of a monkey of yours!'

'Don't you like him?' said Tinker, sorrowfully. 'He likes you.'

Joanna glanced across at the tiny monkey. He sat huddled in a corner, his arms over his face, looking very small and sad. One small brown eye peeped out at Joanna.

'You're a humbug, you are!' said Joanna. 'Looking as if you're the unhappiest monkey in the world, when all the time you're thinking what mischief to do next. Here – come and get this biscuit, you rascal – and don't you dare to go near Timmy this morning. He's very, very angry with you.'

'What did Mischief do to Timmy?' asked Tinker, surprised.

'He went to Timmy's dish and stole one of the bones there,' said Joanna. 'Timmy growled like a roll of thunder! I really thought he would bite off the monkey's tail. My word, you should have seen Mischief skedaddle!'

Mischief had now crept up cautiously to Joanna, eyeing the biscuit she held. He had had one or two slaps from her for stealing, and he was rather wary of her quick right hand.

'Here you are – take the biscuit, for goodness sake,' said Joanna. 'And don't look such a little misery, or I might suddenly find myself giving you another biscuit. Hallo – where's he gone?'

The monkey had snatched the biscuit with one of his tiny paws, and had scampered away to the door. It was shut, so Tinker opened it for him. At once Timmy came in. He had been lying outside the door, sniffing the good smell of soup cooking on the stove.

Mischief leapt to the top of a chair back and made a strange little whinnying sound – rather apologetic and sad. Timmy stood still and pricked up his ears. He understood animal language very well!

Mischief still held the biscuit. He leapt down to the seat of the chair – and then, to Joanna's enormous surprise, he held out the biscuit to Timmy! He chattered in a very small voice, and Timmy listened gravely. Then the big dog took the biscuit gently, threw it into the air, chewed it once, and swallowed it!

'Well, did you ever see anything like that before!' said Joanna, marvelling. 'For all the world as if Mischief was apologising to Timmy for stealing his bone – and offering him his biscuit to make up! Well, whatever will George say when she hears!'

Timmy licked his lips to see if any biscuit crumbs were left, and then put his big head forward, and gave the monkey a sudden lick on the tip of his funny little nose.

From **FIVE GO TO DEMON'S ROCKS**

THE COTTAGE ON THE HILL – AND WILFRID

THEY LEFT their bicycles in a heap and went through the gate. Not far to their left stood a funny old cottage, its back to them, its front looking down the steep hill that ran towards the great harbour and the sea beyond.

'It's like a cottage out of an old fairy-tale,' said Anne. 'Funny little chimneys, rather crooked walls, a thatched roof, all uneven – and what tiny windows!'

They walked down a little winding path that led to the cottage. They soon came to a well, and leant over it to see the water deep down. 'So that's the water we'd have to drink!' said Anne, wrinkling up her nose. 'And we'd have to let down the bucket by winding this handle – and down it would go on the rope! Do you suppose the water is pure?'

'Well, seeing that people must have drunk it for years on end – the ones living in that cottage, anyway – I should imagine it's all right!' said Julian. 'Come on – let's find the front door of the cottage – if it has one!'

It had a wooden door, hung rather crooked, with an old brass knocker. It faced down the hill, and was flanked on each side by small windows. Two other small windows were above. Julian looked at them. 'The bedrooms would be very small,' he thought. 'Would there really be room for them all?'

He knocked at the door. Nobody came to open it. He knocked again, and then looked for a bell, but there wasn't one.

'See if the door is unlocked,' said Anne. So Julian turned the handle – and at once the door gave under his hand! It opened straight into a room that looked like a kitchen-living room.

Julian gave a shout. 'Anyone at home?'

There was no answer. 'Well – as this is obviously the cottage we were meant to see, we'd better go in,' said Julian and they all went.

It was old – very old. The carved wooden furniture was old too. Ancient oil lamps stood on two tables in the room, and in a recess there was an oil stove with a saucepan on top. A narrow, crooked stairway made of wood curved up to the floor above. Julian went up, and found himself in a long, darkish room, its roof thatched with reed and held up by black beams.

'This place must be hundreds of years old!' he called down to the others. 'I don't think it's big enough for us four and the others too – Wilfrid and the helper.'

Just as he finished calling down the stairs, the front door was flung open and someone came in.

'What are you doing here?' he shouted. 'This is my cottage!'

Julian went quickly down the stairs, and there, facing them all, stood a boy of about ten, a scowl on his brown face.

'Er – are you Wilfrid, by any chance?' asked Dick, politely.

'Yes, I am. And who are you? And where's my grandmother? She'll soon chuck you out!' said the boy.

'Is your grandmother Mrs Layman?' asked Julian. 'If so, she asked us to come and see her cottage, and decide if we'd like to keep you company. She said she had to go away and look after a sick relative.'

'Well, I don't want you!' said the boy. 'So clear off. I'm all right here alone. My grandmother's a nuisance, always fussing around.'

'I thought there was a lady who looks after you too,' said Julian. 'Where is she?'

'She only comes in the morning, and I sent her off,' said Wilfrid. 'She left me some food. I want to be alone. I don't want you. So clear off.'

'Don't be an idiot, Wilfrid,' said Julian. 'You can't live all alone here. You're just a kid.'

'I shan't be living all alone. I've plenty of friends,' said Wilfrid, defiantly.

'You can't have plenty of friends here in this lonely place, with only the hills and sky around you,' said Dick.

'Well, I have!' said Wilfrid. 'And here's one – so look out!' And, to the horror of the two girls, he put his hand into his pocket, and brought out a snake!

Anne screamed, and tried to hide behind Julian. Wilfrid saw her fright and came towards her, holding the snake by its middle, so that it swayed to and fro, its bright little eyes gleaming.

'Don't be scared, Anne,' said Julian. 'It's only a harmless grass snake. Put the creature back into your pocket, Wilfrid, and don't play the fool. If that snake is the only friend you have, you'll be pretty lonely here by yourself!'

'I've plenty of friends, I tell you!' shouted Wilfrid, stuffing the snake back into his pocket. 'I'll hit you if you don't believe me.'

'Oh no, you won't,' said Dick. 'Just show us your other friends. If they're kids like you, it's just too bad!'

'Kids? I don't make friends with kids!' said Wilfrid, scornfully. 'I'll show you I'm speaking the truth. Come out here on the hillside, and see some of my other friends.'

They all trooped out of the little cottage, on to the hillside, amazed at this fierce, strange boy. When they were in the open, they saw that he had eyes as bright blue as the speedwell in the grass, and hair almost as yellow as the celandines.

'Sit down and keep quiet,' he ordered. 'Over there, by that bush. And don't move a finger. I'll soon make you believe in my friends! How dare you come here, doubting my word!'

They all sat down obediently beside the gorse bush, puzzled and rather amused. The boy sat down too, and drew something out of his pocket. What was it? George tried to see, but it was half-hidden in his right hand.

He put it to his mouth, and began to whistle. It was a soft, weird whistle that grew loud and then died away again. There was no tune, no melody, just a kind of beautiful dirge that pulled at the heart. 'Sad,' thought Anne. 'Such a sad little tune – if you could call it a tune!'

Something stirred a little way down the hill – and then to everyone's astonishment, an animal appeared – a hare! Its great ears stood upright, its big eyes stared straight at the boy with the curious little pipe. Then the hare lolloped right up to Wilfrid – and began to dance! Soon another came, but this one only watched. The first one then seemed to go mad, and leapt about wildly, utterly unafraid.

The tune changed a little – and a rabbit appeared. Then another and another. One came to Wilfrid's feet and sniffed at them, its whiskers quivering. Then it lay down against the boy's foot.

A bird flew down – a beautiful magpie! It stood nearby, watching the hare, fascinated. It took no notice of the children at all. They all held their breath, amazed and delighted.

And then Timmy gave a little growl, deep down in his throat. He didn't really mean to, but he just couldn't help it! At once the hares, the rabbits and the magpie fled, the magpie squawking in fright.

Wilfrid faced round at once, his eyes blazing. He lifted his hand to strike Timmy – but George caught his fist at once.

'Let go!' yelled Wilfrid. 'That dog scared my friends! I'll get a stick and whip him. He's the worst dog in the world, he's . . .'

And then something strange happened. Timmy came gently over to Wilfrid, lay down, and put his head on the angry boy's knee, looking up at him lovingly. The boy, his hand still raised to strike, lowered it, and fondled Timmy's head, making a curious crooning noise.

'Timmy! Come here!' ordered George, amazed and angry. To think that her dog, her very own dog, should go to a boy who had been about to strike him! Timmy stood up, gave Wilfrid a lick, and went to George.

TINKER AND MISCHIEF AGAIN!

THE FOUR children and Timmy went through the big heavy gate, which groaned loudly. Timmy was very startled to hear the mournful creak, and barked sharply.

'Sh!' said George. 'You'll get into trouble with the Professor, Timmy, if you raise your voice like that. I expect we'll have to talk in whispers, so as not to disturb the Professor – so just see if you can whisper too.'

Timmy gave a small whine. He knew he couldn't whisper! He trotted at George's heel as they all went down the steep drive to the house. It was a curious house, built sideways to the drive, and had astonishingly few windows.

'I expect Professor Hayling is afraid of people peering in at his work,' said Anne. 'It's very, very secret, isn't it?'

'I know he uses miles and miles of figures,' said Dick. 'Tinker told me one day that his monkey Mischief once chewed up a page of figures when he was very small – and Professor Hayling chased him for a whole hour, hoping to catch him and find even a few bits of paper still in his mouth, so that he could rescue at least part of his figures. But Mischief fled down a rabbit hole and didn't come up for two days, so it wasn't any good.'

Everyone smiled at the thought of poor Mischief hiding down a rabbit hole. 'You couldn't do that, Timmy old thing!' said Julian. 'So just be careful of any paper you eat.'

'He wouldn't be so silly,' said George, at once. 'He knows perfectly well what's eatable and what's not.'

'Ha! Does he?' said Anne. 'Well, I'd just like to know what kind of food he thought my blue slipper was that he chewed up last hols!'

'Don't tell tales on him,' said George. 'He only chewed it because someone shut him in your bedroom and he hadn't anything else to do.'

'Woof,' said Timmy, quite agreeing. He gave Anne's hand a little lick, as if to say, 'Very sorry, Anne – but I was so bored!'

'Dear Timmy! I wouldn't mind if you chewed up all my slippers!' said Anne. 'But it would be nice if you chose the very oldest ones!'

Timmy suddenly stopped and looked into the bushes. He gave a low growl! George put her hand on his collar at once. She was always afraid of snakes in the springtime.

'It might be an adder!' she said. 'The dog next door trod on one last year, so I heard, and his leg swelled up terribly, and he was in great pain. Come away now, Timmy – it's an adder, with poison in its fangs!'

But Timmy went on growling. Then he suddenly stood still and sniffed hard. He gave an excited whimper and pulled away from George, jumping into the bushes – and out came, not a snake, but Mischief, Tinker's bright-eyed little monkey!

He at once leapt on to the dog's broad back, put his little monkey fingers under Timmy's collar, and chattered in delight. Timmy nearly dislocated his neck to twist his head round to lick him!

'Mischief!' cried everyone at once, in real delight. 'You've come to welcome us!'

And the little monkey, jabbering away excitedly in monkey language, leapt first on to George's shoulder, and then on to Julian's. He pulled Julian's hair, twisted his right ear round, and then leapt from him to Dick, and on to Anne's shoulder. He cuddled into her neck, his eyes bright and brown, looking very happy.

'Oh! Isn't he pleased to see us again!' said Anne, delighted. 'Mischief, where's Tinker?'

Mischief jumped off Anne's shoulder and scampered down the drive as if he quite understood all that Anne had said. The children raced after him – and then a loud voice suddenly roared at them from one side of the drive.

'What are you doing here? Clear out! This is private ground. I'll fetch the police. Clear OUT!'

The Five stopped still in fright – and then Julian saw who it was – Professor Hayling! He stepped forward at once. 'Good afternoon,' he said. 'I hope we didn't disturb you, but you did tell my aunt we could come here.'

'Your aunt? Who's your aunt? I don't know any aunt!' roared the Professor. 'You're sightseers, that's what you are! Come to pry into my work, just because there was a piece about it in some silly paper! You're the third lot today. Clear out, I tell you – and take that dog too. How DARE you!'

'But – don't you really know us?' said Julian very startled. 'You came to stay at our house, you know, and . . .'

'Stuff and nonsense! I haven't been away for years!' shouted the Professor. Mischief, the monkey, was so frightened that he leapt away into the bushes, making a funny little crying noise.

'I hope he fetches Tinker,' said Julian, in a low voice to Dick. 'The Professor has forgotten who we are, and why we've come. Let's retreat a bit.'

But as they went cautiously back up the steep path, followed by the angry Professor, a loud voice hailed them, and Tinker came racing up with Mischief on his shoulder, clinging to his hair. So the little monkey had gone to fetch him. 'Good for him!' thought Julian, pleased.

'Dad! Don't yell at our friends like that!' cried Tinker, dancing about in front of his angry father. 'You asked them here yourself, you know you did!'

'I DID NOT!' said the Professor. 'Who are they?'

'Well, George, that girl, is the daughter of Mr Kirrin, and the others are his niece and nephews. And that's their dog, Timmy. And you asked them all here because Mr and Mrs Kirrin are in quarantine for scarlet fever,' shouted Tinker, still dancing about in front of his father.

'Stop jigging about like that,' said the Professor, crossly. 'I don't remember asking them. I would have told Jenny the housekeeper if I had.'

'You did tell her!' shouted Tinker, still jigging about, with Mischief the monkey jigging too in delight. 'She's angry because you left your breakfast and now it's almost dinner-time. She's cleared it away.'

'Bless us – so that's why I feel so hungry and cross!' said Professor Hayling, and he began to laugh. He had a tremendous laugh, and the children couldn't help laughing too. What an odd fellow – so brainy, such a fine scientist – with the most enormous amount of knowledge in his head – and yet no memory for such ordinary things as breakfast and visitors and telephone calls.

'It was just a misunderstanding,' said Julian, politely. 'It was very, very kind of you to invite us here when we can't be at home because of the scarlet fever. We'll try not to be a nuisance, and if there's anything we can do to help you, please ask us. We'll make as little noise as possible, and keep out of your way, of course.'

'You hear that, Tinker?' said Professor Hayling, suddenly swinging round on the startled Tinker. 'Why can't you do the same – make very little noise, and keep out of my way? You know I'm very busy now – on a most important project.' He turned to Julian. 'You'll be very welcome if you keep Tinker out of my way. And nobody – absolutely nobody – is to go up into that tower. Understand?'

They all looked up to where he was pointing, and saw a tall, slender tower rising up amid the trees. It had curious tentacle-like rods sticking out at the top, and these shook slightly in the breeze.

'And don't ask me questions about it,' went on the Professor, looking fiercely at George. 'Your father's the only other man who knows what it's for, and he knows how to keep his mouth shut.'

'None of us would dream of prying,' said Julian. 'It's very, very kind of you to offer to have us here, and do believe me when I say we shan't be any trouble to you at all – but a help if you'll allow us.'

'Ah well, you sound a sensible fellow, I must say,' said the Professor, who had now calmed down, and looked quite peaceable. 'Well, I'll say goodbye for now and go and have my breakfast. I hope it's fried eggs and bacon. I'm very hungry.'

'Dad – Jenny's cleared your breakfast away! I told you that before!' said Tinker in despair. 'It's almost dinner-time, now.'

'Ah good – good!' said the Professor. 'I'll come at once.'

And he led the way indoors, followed by the five children, with Timmy and Mischief, all looking rather worried. Really, nobody ever knew what the Professor was going to do or say next!

Jenny certainly had a good dinner for them all. There was a large and delicious stew with carrots, onions and peas swimming in the gravy, and plenty of potatoes. Everyone tucked in well, and Mischief, who loved the peas, took quite a few from Tinker's plate, his little paw creeping up and neatly snatching a pea from the gravy.

The girls went out to help bring in the next course, which was a big steamed pudding with plenty of raisins in it. Mischief at once jigged up and down in delight, for he loved raisins. He leapt on to the table, and received a sharp smack from the Professor, who unfortunately smacked the pudding dish at the same time, making the pudding jump in the air.

'Good gracious, Dad – we nearly lost the pudding!' cried Tinker. 'And it's my favourite. Oh, don't give us such small pieces! Mischief, get off the table. You are NOT to put your paw into the sauce!'

So Mischief disappeared under the table, where he received quite a lot of raisins from various kindly hands, unseen by the Professor. Timmy felt rather left out. He was under the table too, having been rather scared by the Professor's angry voice, but as he didn't very much like raisins, he wasn't as lucky as Mischief.

'Ha – I enjoyed that!' said the Professor, having cleaned his plate thoroughly. 'Nothing like a good breakfast!'

'It was midday dinner, Dad!' said Tinker. 'You don't have pudding at breakfast.'

from **FIVE ARE TOGETHER AGAIN**

AS SOON as Jeremy saw the visitors climbing over the fence, he ran to help them. He was very excited at the thought of having guests. He took them over to old Grandad first, to be welcomed.

'Now I expect your friends will like to see round a bit,' said Grandad. 'Charlie the Chimp can go with you. We've a rehearsal on tonight, so the ring has been set up. You can watch some of the show.'

This was great news. The children saw that curved pieces of painted wood had been set together to make a great ring in the field, and as they went across the grass, the Musical Horses began to troop into the ring, the leading one ridden by Madelon, a lovely girl dressed in shimmering gold.

'How beautiful they are!' thought Anne, as she watched. 'Look at their great feathery plumes, nodding on their magnificent heads.'

The Bonzo Band struck up just then, and the horses at once trotted in perfect time to the music. The band looked a little peculiar as the bandsmen had not put on their smart uniforms. They were saving those for the opening night!

The horses trotted prettily out of the ring after two or three rounds, the beautiful Madelon on the leading horse. Then in came Fred the Fiddler and played his violin for a few minutes. First the music was slow and solemn, then Fred began to play quickly, and the children found themselves jigging about, up and down and round about. 'I can't keep still!' panted Anne. 'The tune's got into my feet.'

Charlie the Chimp came up just then, walking on hind legs, and looking unexpectedly tall. He usually walked on all fours. He began to jig about too, looking very funny. He ran right into the ring and put his arms round Fred the Fiddler's legs. 'He loves Fred,' said Jeremy. 'Now he's going to rehearse his cricket act. I must go and bowl to him.'

And off went Jeremy into the ring. The chimpanzee rushed over to him and hugged him. A bat was thrown into the ring, and Charlie picked it up and made a few swipes into the air with it, making delighted noises all the time.

Then a cricket ball was thrown to Jeremy, who caught it deftly. A small girl appeared from somewhere and set up three stumps for a wicket. 'Can't find the bails, Jeremy!' she called. 'Have you got them in your pocket?'

'No,' said Jeremy. 'Never mind, I'll knock the stumps right over!'

But that wasn't so easy with Charlie the Chimp at the wicket! He took a terrific swipe at the ball and it went right over Jeremy's head, too high to catch. The chimp lost his balance and sat down on the wicket, knocking the stumps out of the ground.

'OUT!' yelled Jeremy, but the chimp wasn't having that. He carefully put up the stumps again, and then set himself in front once more, waggling the bat.

It was the funniest cricket that the children had ever seen! The chimpanzee was very, very clever with the bat, and sent poor Jeremy running all over the place. Then he chased the boy all round the ring with the bat, making curious chortling noises. The children didn't know if he was amused or angry! Finally he threw the bat at Jeremy and walked off, scratching himself under one arm.

The children roared with laughter at him. 'He's as good as any clown!' said Dick. 'Jeremy, does he do this cricket act every night when the circus is open?'

'Oh yes – and sometimes he hits the ball into the audience,' said Jeremy. 'There's great excitement then. Sometimes, for a treat, we let one of the boys in the audience come down and bowl to Charlie. One bowled him right out once, and Charlie was so cross that he chased him all round the ring three times – just as he chased me just now. The boy didn't like it much!'

Charlie came up to Jeremy and put his great arms round him, trying to swing him off the ground. 'Stop that, Charlie,' said Jeremy, wriggling free. 'Look out – here comes the Dancing Donkey! Better get out of the ring – goodness knows what antics he'll be up to!'

In came the Dancing Donkey. He was dark grey, and tossed his head as he came galloping in. He stood and looked round at everyone. Then he sat down, lifted up a leg and scratched his nose. The children stared in astonishment. They had never in their lives seen a donkey do that before! Then, when the band suddenly began to play, the donkey stood up and listened, flapping his ears first one way and then another, and nodding his head in time to the music.

The band changed its tune to a march. The donkey listened again, and then began to march round the ring in perfect time – clip-clop-clip-clop-clip-clop. Then it apparently felt tired, and sat down heavily on its back legs. The children couldn't help laughing. The donkey got up, and somehow its back legs became entangled with its front ones and it fell down, looking most ridiculous.

'Has it hurt itself?' asked Anne, anxiously. 'Oh dear – it will break one of its legs if it goes on like this. Look, it can't untangle them, Jeremy.'

The donkey gave a mournful bray, tried to get up, and flopped down again. The band changed its tune, and the donkey leapt up at once, and began to do a kind of tap dance – clickety-click, clickety-click, clickety-click – it was marvellous!

'I shouldn't have thought that a donkey could possibly have been taught to tap dance,' said George.

Soon the donkey seemed to feel tired again. It stopped dancing, but the band still went on playing. The donkey ran towards it and stamped a foot.

A weird voice suddenly came from it. 'Too fast! TOO FAST!' But the band took no notice and went on playing. The donkey bent down, wriggled hard – and its head fell off on to the grass in the ring! Anne gave a shriek of fright.

'Don't be an idiot, Anne,' said Dick. 'You didn't think the donkey was a real one, did you?'

'Isn't it?' said Anne, relieved. 'It looks just like that donkey that used to give rides to children on Kirrin beach.'

The donkey now split in half and a small man climbed out of each half, both taking their legs carefully out of the donkey's legs. The donkey-skin fell to the ground and lay there, flat and collapsed.

'Wish I had a donkey-skin like that,' said Tinker. 'I've got a friend at school who could be the back legs and I'd be the front legs. The things we'd do!'

'Well, I must say you'd make a first-class donkey, the way you behave sometimes,' said George.

from FIVE ARE TOGETHER AGAIN

TRAINING YOUR PET

If you long to own a dog to be your constant devoted companion, as Timmy is to George, make sure you're well prepared for this big commitment.

Training should begin as soon as your puppy arrives home. It's much easier to start right away than try to undo bad habits later. Make sure everyone in the family sticks to the same rules, otherwise you will just confuse your new pet.

In the wild, dogs live in packs. Pack leaders eat first and sleep in the best spots, so if you feed your dog from the table while you're eating and let him sleep on your bed or lie on the sofa, you are giving the message that your dog is a top member of the pack. This could make life difficult when your cute puppy grows into a teenager and starts trying to take control.

Training should be based on praise and rewards, not punishments. Start with very simple commands and wait until your pet has mastered these before moving on. It can be useful to keep puppies on a lead during training, so they can't get distracted and wander off. Body language means more to dogs than words, so accompany your command with a hand signal and make sure everyone uses the same word and sign. Single words are best, so say 'Sit' rather than 'Sit down', and 'Come' instead of 'Come here'.

CALLING NAMES

It's good to start by teaching puppies their names. Call your pet's name and hold up a treat close to your face. When you have your puppy's full concentration, hand over the treat and make a fuss of your dog. Continue this training, using treats, toys and praise, until you get your pet's attention whenever you call.

SIT!

Next it's a good idea to teach your puppy to sit. This will make grooming and putting on a collar and lead much easier. Apart from this, a dog that sits on command won't jump up at visitors and can be made to sit and wait at the kerb until it is safe to cross the road.

First get your puppy's attention. Hold a treat close to the dog's nose and then move it up and backwards. As the head follows the treat, the legs should bend and your pet will sit down. As the puppy is carrying out the movement say the word 'Sit', then hand over the treat the second your dog's bottom touches the floor. Pushing your puppy's bottom down is not a good idea because your pet may expect you to do this every time.

COME!

Teaching your puppy to come when called is one of the most important training exercises. It could save your dog's life in a dangerous situation, and it will certainly save you a lot of running about, chasing after your pet!

You can either teach this with two people, where one leads the dog away and the other calls his or her name, or on your own by holding your dog on a long lead, then calling your pet. Use the simple command 'Come'. Gradually increase the distance, then try the exercise with the dog running free. Dogs should be rewarded as soon as they come back, so that they associate coming back to you with something nice.

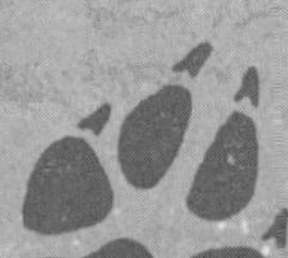

GET TO KNOW DICK

Dick is Julian and Anne's eleven-year-old brother. He's the same age as George. When he was little he was a bit of a cry-baby, but he has grown into a brave and resourceful boy.

Don't be surprised if it's Dick who spots the clue or detail that leads to solving a mystery. He can still be a joker, though, and has a great sense of humour. You'll sometimes find him making fun of Julian when he's being too serious, and he's good at winning over George – although sometimes he also deliberately says things to annoy George in order to provoke her famous frown!

Dick is usually hungry and does not like to miss a meal. Perhaps it's because of him that wonderful food features so often in the books.

Dick says

Let's have our dinner!

I wonder what sort of a tutor Uncle Quentin will choose. If only he would choose the right kind – someone jolly and full of fun, who knows that holiday lessons are sickening to have, and tries to make up for them by being a sport out of lesson-time.

Other people say

You're a brick! A real brick!

TRAVELS with THE FAMOUS FIVE

FIVE AND A HALF-TERM ADVENTURE

The Five were at Kirrin Cottage for a short half-term holiday. For once, both the boys' school and the girls' school had chosen the same weekend!

'It hardly ever happens that we can spend half-term together,' said Anne, fondling Timmy. 'And what luck to have such lovely weather at the beginning of November!'

'Four days off!' said George. 'What shall we do?'

'BATHE!' said Julian and Dick together.

'What!' said their aunt, horrified. 'Bathe in November! You must be mad! I can't allow that, Julian, really I can't.'

'All right,' said Julian, grinning at his aunt. 'Don't worry. We haven't got our swimsuits here.'

'Let's walk over to Windy Hill,' said Dick. 'It's a grand walk, by the sea most of the way. And there may be blackberries and nuts still to find. I'd like a good walk.'

'Woof,' said Timmy at once, and put his big paw up on Dick's knee. He was always hoping to hear that magic word 'Walk!'

'Yes, let's do that,' said Anne. 'Aunt Fanny, shall we take a picnic lunch – or it is too much bother to prepare?'

'Not if you help me,' said her aunt, getting up. 'Come along – we'll see what we can find. But remember that it gets dark very quickly in the afternoon now, so don't leave it too late when you turn back.'

The Five set off half an hour later, with sandwiches and slices of fruit cake in a knapsack carried by Julian. Dick had a basket for any nuts or blackberries. His aunt had promised a blackberry-and-apple pie if they did find any berries for picking.

Timmy was very happy. He trotted along with the others, sniffing here and there, and barking at a curled-up hedgehog in a hole in a bank.

'Now, leave it alone,' said George. 'You really should have learnt by now that hedgehogs are not meant to be carried in your mouth, Timmy! Don't wake it up – it's gone to sleep for the winter!'

'It's a heavenly day for the beginning of November,' said Anne. 'The trees still have their leaves – all colours: red, yellow, brown, pink – and the beeches are the colour of gold.'

'Blackberries!' said Dick, catching sight of a bush whose sprays were still covered with the black fruit. 'I say – taste them – they're as sweet as sugar!'

As soon as the blackberries were to be seen on bushes here and there, the Five slowed up considerably! The blackberries that were still left were big and full of sweetness.

'They melt in my mouth!' said George. 'Try one, Timmy!' But Timmy spat the blackberry out in disgust.

'Manners, Timmy, manners!' said Dick at once, and Timmy wagged his big tail and pranced round joyfully.

It was a good walk but a slow one. They found a hazelnut copse and filled the basket with nuts that had fallen to the ground. Two red squirrels sat up in a nearby tree and chattered at them crossly. This was their nut copse!

'You can spare us a few!' called Anne. 'I expect you've got hundreds hidden away safely for the winter.'

They had their lunch on the top of Windy Hill. It was not a windy day, but, all the same, there was a good breeze on the top, and Julian decided to sit behind a big gorse bush for shelter. 'We'll be in the sun and out of the wind then,' he said. 'Spread out the lunch, Anne!'

'I feel terribly hungry!' said George. 'I can't believe it's only just one o'clock, Julian.'

'Well, that's what my watch says,' said Julian, taking a sandwich. 'Ha – ham

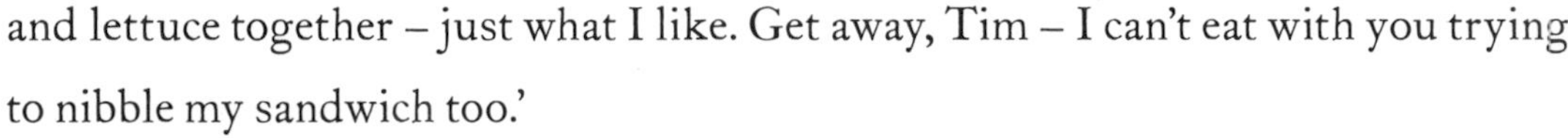

and lettuce together – just what I like. Get away, Tim – I can't eat with you trying to nibble my sandwich too.'

It was a magnificent view from the top of the hill. The four children munched their sandwiches and gazed down into the valley below. A town lay there, comfortably sprawled in the shelter of the hills. Smoke rose lazily from the chimneys.

'Look – there's a train running along the railway line down there,' said George, waving her sandwich in its direction. 'It looks just like a toy one.'

'It's going to Beckton,' said Julian. 'See – there's the station – it's stopping there. It really does look like a toy train!'

'Now it's off again – on its way to Kirrin, I suppose,' said Dick. 'Any more sandwiches? What, none? Shame! I'll have a slice of cake, then – hand over, Anne.'

They talked lazily, enjoying being together again. Timmy wandered from one to the other, getting a titbit here and a scrap of ham there.

'I think I can see another nut copse over yonder – the other side of the hill,' said George. 'I vote we go and see what nuts we can find – and then I suppose we ought to be thinking of going back home. The sun is getting awfully low, Ju.'

'Yes, it is, considering it's only about two o'clock,' said Julian, looking at the red November sun hardly showing above the horizon. 'Come on, then – let's get a few more nuts, and then go back home. I love that long path winding over the cliffs beside the sea.'

They all went off to the little copse, and to their delight, found a fine crop of hazelnuts there. Timmy nosed about in the grass and brought mouthfuls of the nuts to George.

'Thanks, Timmy,' said George. 'Very clever of you – but I wish you could tell the bad ones from the good ones!'

'I say,' said Dick, after a while, 'the sun's gone, and it's getting dark. Julian, are you sure your watch is right?'

Julian looked at his watch. 'It says just about two o'clock still,' he said in surprise. 'Gosh – I must have forgotten to wind it up or something. It's definitely stopped now – and it must have been very slow before!'

'Idiot,' said Dick. 'No wonder George thought it was long past lunch-time when you said it was one o'clock. We'll never get home before dark now – and we haven't any torches with us.'

'That cliff path isn't too good to walk along in the dark, either,' said Anne. 'It goes so near the edge at times.'

'We'd better start back immediately,' said Julian. 'Awfully sorry about this – I never dreamed that my watch was wrong.'

'I tell you what would be a better idea,' said George. 'Why don't we just take the path down into Beckton and catch the train to Kirrin? We'll be so late if we walk back, and Mother will be ringing up the police about us!'

'Good idea of yours, George,' said Julian. 'Come on – let's take the path while we can still see. It leads straight down to the town.'

So away went the Five as fast as they could. It was dark when they reached the town, but that didn't matter, because the streetlamps were alight. The made their way to the station, half-running down the main street.

'Look – there's Robin Hood on at the cinema here,' said Anne. 'Look at the posters!'

'And what's that on at the hall over there?' said George. 'Timmy, come here – oh, he's shot across the road. Come HERE, Timmy!'

But Timmy was running up the steps of the Town Hall. Julian gave a sudden laugh. 'Look – there's a big dog show on there – and old Timmy must have thought he ought to go in for it!'

'He smelt the dogs there,' said George, rather cross. 'Come on – let's get him, or we'll lose the next train.'

The hall was plastered with posters of dogs of all kinds. Julian stopped to read

them while George went in after Timmy.

'Some jolly valuable dogs here,' he said. 'Some beauties, too – look at the picture of this white poodle. Ah – here comes Tim again, looking very sorry for himself. I bet he knows he wouldn't win a single prize – except for brains!'

'It was the doggy smell that made him go to see what was on,' said George. 'He was awfully cross because they wouldn't let him in.'

'Hurry up – I think I can hear a train coming!' said Dick, and they all raced down the road to the station, which was quite near.

The train puffed in as they went to the booking office for their tickets. The guard was blowing his whistle and waving his flag as they rushed on to the platform. Dick pulled open the door of the very last compartment and they all bundled in, panting.

'Gosh – that was a near squeak,' said Dick, half-falling on to a seat. 'Look out, Tim – you nearly had me over.'

The four children got back their breath and looked round the carriage. It was not empty, as they had expected. Two other people were there, sitting at the opposite end, facing each other – a man and a woman. They looked at the Five, annoyed.

'Oh,' said Anne, seeing the woman carrying a shawled bundle in her arms, 'I hope we haven't woken your baby. We only just caught the train.'

The woman rocked the little thing in her arms, and crooned to it, covering its head with a shawl – a rather dirty one, Anne noticed.

'Is she all right?' asked the man. 'Cover her up more – it's cold in here.'

'There, there now,' crooned the woman, pulling the shawl tighter. The children lost interest and began to talk. Timmy sat still by George, very bored. Then he suddenly sniffed round, and went over to the woman. He leapt up on to the seat beside her and pawed at the shawl!

The woman shrieked and the man shouted at Timmy.

'Stop that! Get down! Here, you kids, look after that great dog of yours. It'll frighten the baby into fits!'

'Come here, Timmy,' said George at once, surprised that he should be interested in a baby. Timmy whined and went to George, looking back at the woman. A tiny whimpering noise came from the shawl, and the woman frowned. 'You've waked her,' she said, and began to talk to the man in a loud, harsh voice.

Timmy was very disobedient! Before George could stop him, he was up on the seat again, pawing at the woman and whining. The man leapt up furiously.

'Don't hit my dog, don't hit him, he'll snap at you!' shouted George – and mercifully, just at that moment the train drew in at a station.

'Let's get out and go into another carriage,' said Anne, and opened the door. The four of them, followed by a most unwilling Timmy, were soon getting into a compartment near the engine. George looked crossly at Timmy.

'Whatever came over you, Tim?' she said. 'You are never interested in babies! Now sit down and don't move!'

Timmy was surprised at George's cross voice, and he crept under the seat and stayed there. The train came to a little station, where there was a small platform, and stopped to let a few people get out.

'It's Seagreen Halt,' said Dick, looking out. 'And there go the man and woman and baby – I must say I wouldn't like them for a Mum and Dad!'

'It's quite dark now,' said George, looking through the window. 'It's a jolly good thing we just caught the train. Mother will be getting worried.'

* * *

It was nice to be in the cosy sitting-room at Kirrin Cottage again, eating an enormous tea and telling George's mother about their walk. She was very pleased with the nuts and blackberries. They told her about the man and woman and baby, too, and how funny Timmy had been, pawing at the shawl.

'He was funny before that,' said Anne, remembering. 'Aunt Fanny, there was a dog show on at Beckton, and Timmy must have read the posters, and thought he could go in for it – because he suddenly dashed across the road and into the Town Hall where the show was being held!'

'Really?' said her aunt, laughing. 'Well, perhaps he went to see if he could find the beautiful little white Pekinese that was stolen there today! Mrs Harris rang up and told me about it – there was such a to-do. The little dog, which was worth £5,000, was cuddled down in its basket one minute – and the next it was gone! Nobody was seen to take it, and though they hunted in every corner of the hall, there was no sign of the dog.'

'Gracious!' said Anne. 'What a mystery! How could anyone possibly take a dog like that away without being seen?'

'Easy,' said Dick. 'Wrap it in a coat, or pop it into a shopping basket and cover it up. Then walk through the crowd and out of the hall!'

'Or wrap it in a shawl and pretend it was a BABY – like the little one in that dirty shawl in the train,' said Anne. 'I mean – we thought that was a baby, of course – but it could easily have been a dog – or a cat – or even a monkey. We couldn't see its face!'

There was a sudden silence. Everyone was staring at Anne and thinking hard. Julian banged his hand on the table and made everyone jump.

'There's something in what Anne has just said,' he said. 'Something worth thinking about! Did anyone see even a glimpse of the baby's face – or hair? Did you, Anne – you were nearest?'

'No,' said Anne, quite startled. 'No, I didn't. I did try to see, because I like babies – but the shawl was pulled right over the face and head.'

'And I say – don't you remember how interested Timmy was in it?' said George, excited. 'He's never interested in babies – but he kept on jumping up and pawing at the shawl.'

'And do you remember how the baby whimpered?' said Dick. 'It was much more like a little dog whining than a baby, now I come to think of it. No wonder Timmy was excited! He knew it was a dog by the smell!'

'Whew! I say – this is jolly exciting,' said Julian, getting up. 'I vote we go to Seagreen Halt and snoop round the tiny village there.'

'No,' said Aunt Fanny firmly. 'I will not have that, Julian. It's as dark as pitch outside, and I don't want you snooping round for dog thieves on your half-term holiday.'

'Oh, I say!' said Julian, bitterly disappointed.

'Ring up the police,' said his aunt. 'Tell them what you have just told me – they'll be able to find out the truth very quickly. They will be sure to know who has a baby and who hasn't – they can go round snooping quite safely!'

'All right,' said Julian, sad to have a promising adventure snatched away so quickly. He went to the phone, frowning. Aunt Fanny might have let him and Dick slip out to Seagreen in the dark – it would have been such fun.

The police were most interested and asked a lot of questions. Julian told them all he knew, and everyone listened intently. Then Julian put down the receiver and turned to the others, looking quite cheerful again.

'They were jolly interested,' he said. 'And they're off to Seagreen Village straight away in the police car. They're going to let us know what they find. Aunt Fanny – we CANNOT go to bed tonight till we know what happens!'

'No, we can't!' cried all the others, and Timmy joined in with a bark, leaping round excitedly.

'Very well,' said Aunt Fanny, smiling. 'What a collection of children you are – you can't even go for a walk without something happening! Now – get out the cards and let's have a game.'

They played cards, with their ears listening for the ringing of the telephone bell. But it didn't ring. Supper time came and still it hadn't rung.

'It's no go, I suppose,' said Dick gloomily. 'We probably made a mistake.'

Timmy suddenly began to bark, and then ran to the door, pawing at it.

'Someone's coming,' said George. 'Listen – it's a car!' They all listened, and heard the car stop at the gate – then footsteps came up the path and the front-door bell rang. George was out in a trice, and opened it.

'Oh – it's the police!' she called. 'Come in, do come in.'

A burly policeman came in, followed by another. The second one carried a bundle in a shawl! Timmy leapt up to it at once, whining!

'Oh! It wasn't a baby, then!' cried Anne, and the policeman smiled and shook his head. He pulled the shawl away – and there, fast asleep, was a tiny white Pekinese, its little snub nose tucked into the shawl!

'Oh – the darling!' said Anne. 'Wake up, you funny little thing!'

'It's been doped,' said the policeman. 'I suppose they were afraid of it whining in the night and giving its hiding place away!'

'Tell us what happened,' begged Dick. 'Get down, Timmy. George, he's getting too excited – he wants the Peke to play with him!'

'Acting on your information we went to Seagreen,' said the policeman. 'We asked the porter what people got out of the train this evening, and if anyone carried a baby – and he said four people got out – and two of them were a man and woman, and the woman carried a baby in a shawl. He told us who they were – so away we went to the cottage . . .'

'Woof,' said Timmy interrupting, trying to get at the tiny dog again, but nobody took any notice of him.

'We looked through the back window of the cottage,' went on the policeman, 'and spotted what we wanted at once! The woman was giving the dog a drink of milk in a saucer – and she must have put some drug into it, because the little thing dropped down and fell asleep at once while we were watching.'

'So in we went, and that was that,' said the second policeman, smiling round. 'The couple were so scared that they blurted out everything – how someone had paid them to steal the dog, and how they had taken their own baby's shawl, wrapped round a cushion – and had stolen the dog quite easily when the judging of the Alsatians was going on. They wrapped the tiny dog in the shawl, just as you thought, and caught the next train home!'

'I wish I'd gone to Seagreen Village with you,' said Julian. 'Do you know who told the couple to steal the little dog?'

'Yes – we're off to interview him now! He'll be most surprised to see us,' said the burly policeman. 'We've informed the owner that we've got her prize dog all right – but she feels so upset about it she can't collect it till the morning – so we wondered if you'd like to keep it for the night? Your Timmy can guard it, can't he?'

'Oh yes,' said George in delight. 'Oh, Mother – I'll take it to my room when I go to bed, and Timmy can guard the tiny thing as much as he likes. He'll love it!'

'Well – if your mother doesn't mind you having two dogs in your room, that's fine!' said the policeman, and signalled to the second one to give George the dog in the shawl. She took it gently, and Timmy leapt up again.

'No, Tim – be careful,' said George. 'Look what a tiny thing it is. You're to guard it tonight.'

Timmy looked at the little sleeping Pekinese, and then, very gently, he licked it with the tip of his pink tongue. This was the tiny dog he had smelt in the train, covered up in the shawl. Oh yes – Timmy had guessed at once!

'I don't know what your name is,' said Dick, stroking the small silky head. 'But I think I'll call you Half-term Adventure, though I don't know what that is in Pekinese!'

The two policemen laughed. 'Well, good night, Madam, good night, children,' said the burly one. 'Mrs Fulton, the dog's owner, will call tomorrow morning for her Peke. He won a £1,000 prize today – so I dare say you'll get some of that for a reward! Good night!'

The Five didn't want a reward, of course – but Timmy had one for guarding the little Peke all night. It's on his neck – the finest studded collar he has ever had in his life! Good old Timmy!

A VISIT TO THE ISLAND

They got into the boat, and George pushed off. The fisher-boy waved to them. 'You won't be very long, will you?' he called. 'There's a storm blowing up. Bad one it'll be, too.'

'I know,' shouted back George. 'But maybe we'll get back before it begins. It's pretty far off yet.'

George rowed all the way to the island. Tim stood at each end of the boat in turn, barking when the waves reared up at him. The children watched the island coming closer and closer. It looked even more exciting than it had the other day.

'George, where are you going to land?' asked Julian. 'I simply can't imagine how you know your way in and out of these awful rocks. I'm afraid every moment we'll bump into them!'

'I'm going to land at the little cove I told you about the other day,' said George. 'There's only one way to it, but I know it very well. It's hidden away on the east side of the island.'

The girl cleverly worked her boat in and out of the rocks, and suddenly, as it rounded a low wall of sharp rocks, the children saw the cove she had spoken of. It was like a natural little harbour, and was a smooth inlet of water running up to a stretch of sand, sheltered between high rocks. The boat slid into the inlet, and at once stopped rocking, for here the water was like glass and had hardly a wrinkle.

'I say – this is fine!' said Julian, his eyes shining with delight. George looked at him and her eyes shone too, as bright as the sea itself. It was the first time she had ever taken anyone to her precious island, and she was enjoying it.

They landed on the smooth yellow sand. 'We're really on the island!' said Anne, and she capered about, Tim joining her and looking as mad as she did.

* * *

Dick fled to the well shaft. Fortunately the opening was on the opposite side, and he could clamber into it without being seen in the light of the torches. The boy only just had time to squeeze through into the shaft before the three men came running by. Not one of them guessed that the runaway was squeezed into the well shaft they passed! Indeed, the men did not even know that there was a well there.

Trembling from head to foot, Dick began to climb the rope he had left dangling from the rungs of the iron ladder. He undid it when he reached the ladder itself, for he thought that perhaps the men might discover the old well and try to climb up later. They would not be able to do that if there was no rope dangling down.

The boy climbed up the ladder quickly, and squeezed round the stone slab near the top. The other children were there, waiting for him.

They knew at once by the look on Dick's face that he had failed in what he had tried to do. They pulled him out quickly. 'It was no good,' said Dick, panting with his climb. 'I couldn't do it. They burst the door open just as I was bolting it, and chased me. I got into the shaft just in time.'

'They're trying to get out of the entrance now!' cried Anne, suddenly. 'Quick! What shall we do? They'll catch us all!'

'To the boat!' shouted Julian, and he took Anne's hand to help her along. 'Come along! It's our only chance. The men will perhaps be able to move those stones.'

The four children fled down the courtyard. George darted into the little stone room as they passed it, and caught up an axe. Dick wondered why she bothered to do that. Tim dashed along with them, barking madly.

They came to the cove. Their own boat lay there without oars. The motorboat was there too. George jumped into it and gave a yell of delight.

'Here are our oars!' she shouted. 'Take them, Julian, I've got a job to do here! Get the boat down to the water, quick!'

Julian and Dick took the oars. Then they dragged their boat down to the water, wondering what George was doing. All kinds of crashing sounds came from the motorboat!

'George! George! Buck up. The men are out!' suddenly yelled Julian. He had seen the three men running to the cliff that led down to the cove. George leapt out of the motorboat and joined the others. They pushed their boat out on to the water, and George took the oars at once, pulling for all she was worth.

The three men ran to their motorboat. Then they paused in the greatest dismay – for George had completely ruined it! She had chopped wildly with her axe at all the machinery she could see – and now the boat could not possibly be started! It was damaged beyond any repair the men could make with the few tools they had.

'You wicked girl!' yelled Jake, shaking his fist at George. 'Wait till I get you!'

'I'll wait!' shouted back George, her blue eyes shining dangerously. 'And you can wait too! You won't be able to leave my island now!'

from **FIVE ON A TREASURE ISLAND**

KIRRIN ISLAND ONCE MORE!

They all clambered into the boat. Timothy leapt in lightly and ran to the prow, where he always stood. His tongue hung out in excitement. He knew quite well that something was up – and he was in it! No wonder he panted and wagged his tail hard.

'Off we go!' said Julian, taking the oars. 'Sit over there a bit, Anne. The luggage is weighing down the boat awfully the other end. Dick, sit by Anne to keep the balance better. That's right. Off we go!'

And off they went in George's boat, rocking up and down on the waves. The sea was fairly calm, but a good breeze blew through their hair. The water splashed round the boat and made a nice gurgly, friendly noise. The children all felt very happy. They were on their own. They were escaping from the horrid Sticks. They were going to stay on Kirrin Island, with the rabbits and gulls and jackdaws.

'Doesn't that new-made bread smell awfully good?' said Dick, feeling very hungry as usual. 'Can we just grab a bit, do you think?'

'Yes, let's,' said George. So they broke off bits of the warm brown crust, handed some to Julian, who was rowing, and chewed the delicious new-made bread. Timmy got a bit too, but his was gone as soon as it went into his mouth.

'Timmy's funny,' said Anne. 'He never eats his food as we do – he seems to drink it – just takes it into his mouth and swallows it, as if it was water!'

The others laughed. 'He doesn't drink his bones,' said George. 'He always eats those all right – chews on them for hours and hours. Don't you, Timothy?'

'Woof!' said Timmy, agreeing. He eyed the place where that enormous bone was, wishing he could have it now. But the children wouldn't let him. They were afraid it might go overboard, and that would be a pity.

'I don't believe anyone has noticed us going,' said Julian. 'Except Alf the fisher-boy, of course. We told him about going to the island, Dick, but nobody else.'

They had called at Alf's house on their way to the cove. Alf was alone in the yard at the back. His mother was away and his father was out fishing. They had told him their secret, and Alf had nodded his tousled head and promised faithfully to tell nobody at all. He was evidently very proud at being trusted.

'If my mother and father come back, you must let us know,' said George. 'Sail as near the island as you dare, and hail us. You can get nearer to it than anyone else.'

'I'll do that,' promised Alf, wishing he could go with them.

'So, you see, Dick,' said Julian, as he rowed out to the island, 'if by any chance Aunt Fanny does return sooner than we expect, we shall know at once and come back. I think we've planned everything very well.'

'Yes, we have,' said Dick. He turned and faced the island, which was coming nearer. 'We shall soon be there. Isn't George going to take the oars and guide the boat in?'

'Yes,' said George. 'We've come to the difficult bit now, where we've got to weave our way in and out of the different rocks that keep sticking up. Give me the oars, Ju.'

She took the oars, and the others watched in admiration as the girl guided the big boat skilfully in and out of the hidden rocks. She certainly was very clever. They felt perfectly safe with her.

The boat slid into the little cove. It was a natural harbour, with the water running up to a stretch of sand. High rocks sheltered it. The children jumped out eagerly, and four pairs of willing hands tugged the boat quickly up the sand.

'Higher up still,' panted George. 'You know what awful storms suddenly blow up in this bay. We want to be sure the boat is quite safe, no matter how high the seas run.'

The boat soon lay on one side, high up the stretch of sand. The children sat down, puffing and blowing. 'Let's have breakfast here,' said Julian. 'I don't feel like unloading all those heavy things at the moment. We'll get what we want for breakfast, and have it here on this warm bit of sand.'

They got a loaf of new bread, some cold ham, a few tomatoes and a pot of jam. Anne found knives and forks and plates. Julian opened two bottles of ginger beer.

'Funny sort of breakfast,' he said, setting the bottles down on the sand, 'but simply gorgeous when anyone is as hungry as we are.'

from FIVE RUN AWAY TOGETHER

THE CARAVANS ARRIVE

At last the great day came when the two caravans were due to arrive. The children stood at the end of the drive for hours, watching for them.

Mother had managed to borrow them from an old friend of hers. The children had promised faithfully to look after them well, and not to damage anything. Now they stood at the end of the drive, watching eagerly for the caravans to arrive.

'They are being drawn by cars today,' said Julian. 'But they are fitted up to be horse-drawn, too. I wonder what they are like – and what colour they are.'

'Will they be like travellers' caravans, on high wheels, do you think?' asked Anne. Julian shook his head.

'No, they're modern, Mother says. Streamlined and all that. Not too big either, because a horse can't draw too heavy a van.'

'They're coming, they're coming! I can see them!' suddenly yelled George, making them all jump. 'Look, isn't that them, far down the road?'

They all looked hard into the distance. No one had such good eyes as George, and all they could see was a blotch, a moving speck far away on the road. But George's eyes saw two caravans, one behind the other.

'George is right,' said Julian, straining his eyes. 'It's our caravans. They're each drawn by a small car.'

'One's red and the other's green,' said Anne. 'Bags I the red one. Oh, hurry up, caravans!'

At last they were near enough to see properly. The children ran to meet them. They certainly were very nice ones, quite modern and 'streamlined', as Julian had said, well built and comfortable.

'They almost reach the ground!' said Anne. 'And look at the wheels, set so neatly into the side of the vans. I do like the red one, bags I the red one.'

Each van had a little chimney, long, narrow windows down the two sides, and tiny ones in front by the driver's seat. There was a broad door at the back and two steps down. Pretty curtains fluttered at the open windows.

'Red curtains for the green caravan, and green ones for the red caravan!' said Anne. 'Oh, I want to go inside!'

But she couldn't because the doors were locked. So she had to be content to run with the others up the drive after the two caravans, shouting loudly:

'Mummy! They're here, the caravans are here.'

Her mother came running down the steps to see. Soon the doors were unlocked and the children went inside the caravans. Delighted shouts came from both vans.

'Bunks along one side – is that where we sleep? How gorgeous!'

'Look at this little sink – we can really wash up. And golly, water comes out of these taps!'

'There's a proper stove to cook on – but I vote we cook out of doors on a camp fire. I say, look at the bright frying-pans – and all the cups and saucers hanging up!'

'It's like a proper little house inside. Doesn't it seem nice and big? Mother, isn't it beautifully planned? Don't you wish you were coming with us?'

'Hey, you girls! Do you see where the water comes from? Out of that tank on the roof. It must collect rainwater. And look at this gadget for heating water. Isn't it all super?'

The children spent hours examining their caravans and finding out all the secrets. They certainly were very well fitted, spotlessly clean and very roomy. George felt as if she couldn't wait to start out. She really must get Dobby and set out at once!

'No, you must wait, silly,' said Julian. 'You know we've to get the other horse. He's not coming till tomorrow.'

The other horse was a sturdy little black fellow called Trotter. He belonged to the milkman, who often lent him out. He was a sensible little horse, and the children

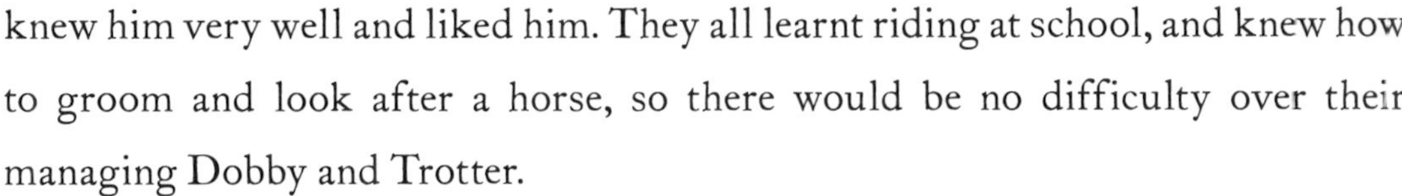

knew him very well and liked him. They all learnt riding at school, and knew how to groom and look after a horse, so there would be no difficulty over their managing Dobby and Trotter.

Mother was thrilled over the caravans, too, and looked very longingly at them. 'If I wasn't going with Daddy I should be most tempted to come with you,' she said. 'Don't look so startled, Anne dear – I'm not really coming!'

'We're jolly lucky to get such decent caravans,' said Julian. 'We'd better pack our things today, hadn't we, Mother – and start off tomorrow, now we've got the caravans.'

'You won't need to pack,' said his mother. 'All you have to do is to pop your things straight into the cupboards and drawers – you will only want clothes and books and a few games to play in case it's rainy.'

'We don't need any clothes except our night things, do we?' said George, who would have lived in a jersey and jeans all day and every day if she had been allowed to.

'You must take plenty of jerseys, another pair of jeans each, in case you get wet, your raincoats, bathing things, towels, a change of shoes, night things and some cool shirts or blouses,' said Mother. Everyone groaned.

'What a frightful lot of things!' said Dick. 'There'll never be room for all those.'

'Oh yes there will,' said Mother. 'You will be sorry if you take too few clothes, get soaked through, have nothing to change into, and catch fearful colds that will stop you from enjoying a lovely holiday like this.'

'Come on, let's get the things,' said Dick. 'Once Mother starts off about catching cold there's no knowing what else she'll make us take – is there, Mother?'

'You're a cheeky boy,' said his mother, smiling. 'Yes, go and collect your things. I'll help you to put them into the cupboards and drawers. Isn't it marvellous how everything folds so neatly into the walls of the caravans – there seems to be room for everything, and you don't notice the cupboards.'

'I shall keep everything very clean,' said Anne. 'You know how I like playing at keeping house, don't you, Mother – well, it will be real this time. I shall have two caravans to keep clean, all by myself.'

'All by yourself!' said her mother. 'Well, surely the boys will help you – and certainly George must.'

'Pooh, the boys!' said Anne. 'They won't know how to wash and dry a cup properly – and George never bothers about things like that. If I don't make the bunks and wash the crockery, they would never be made or washed, I know that!'

'Well, it's a good thing that one of you is sensible!' said her mother. 'You'll find that everyone will share in the work, Anne. Now off you go and get your things. Bring all the raincoats, to start with.'

It was fun taking things down to the caravans and packing them all in. There were shelves for a few books and games, so Julian brought down snap cards, ludo, lexicon, happy families and dominoes, as well as four or five books for each of them. He also brought down some maps of the district, because he meant to plan out where they were to go, and the best roads to follow.

Daddy had given him a useful little book in which were the names of farms that would give permission to caravanners to camp in fields for the night. 'You must always choose a field where there is a stream, if possible,' said his father, 'because Dobby and Trotter will want water.'

'Remember to boil every drop of water you drink,' said the children's mother. 'That's very important. Get as much milk from the farms as they will let you have. And remember that there is plenty of ginger beer in the locker under the second caravan.'

'It's all so thrilling,' said Anne, peering down to look at the locker into which Julian had put the bottles of ginger beer. 'I can't believe we're really going tomorrow.'

But it was true. Dobby and Trotter were to be taken to the caravans the next day and harnessed. How exciting for them, too, Anne thought.

Timmy couldn't quite understand all the excitement, but he shared in it, of course, and kept his tail on the wag all day long. He examined the caravans thoroughly from end to end, found a rug he liked the smell of, and lay down on it. 'This is my corner,' he seemed to say. 'If you go off in these peculiar houses on wheels, this is my own little corner.'

'We'll have the red caravan, George,' said Anne. 'The boys can have the green one. They don't care what colour they have – but I love red. I say, won't it be fun to sleep in those bunks? They look jolly comfortable.'

At last tomorrow came – and the milkman brought the sturdy little black horse, Trotter, up the drive. Julian fetched Dobby from the field. The horses nuzzled one another and Dobby went 'Hrrrumph' in a very civil horsey voice.

'They're going to like each other,' said Anne. 'Look at them nuzzling. Trotter, you're going to draw my caravan.'

The two horses stood patiently while they were harnessed. Dobby jerked his head once or twice as if he was impatient to be off and stamped a little.

'Oh, Dobby, I feel like that, too!' said Anne. 'Don't you, Dick, don't you, Julian?'

'I do rather,' said Dick with a grin. 'Get up there, Dobby – that's right. Who's going to drive, Julian – take it in turns, shall we?'

'I'm going to drive our caravan,' said George. 'Anne wouldn't be any good at it, though I'll let her have a turn at it sometimes. Driving is a man's job.'

'Well, you're only a girl!' said Anne indignantly. 'You're not a man, nor even a boy!'

George put on one of her scowls. She always wanted to be a boy, and even thought of herself as one. She didn't like to be reminded that she was a girl. But not even George could scowl for long that exciting morning! She soon began to caper round and about again, laughing and calling out with the others:

'We're ready! Surely we're ready!'

'Yes. Do let's go! JULIAN! He's gone indoors, the idiot, just when we want to start.'

'He's gone to get the cakes that Cook has baked this morning for us. We've heaps of food in the larder. I feel hungry already.'

'Here's Julian. Do come on, Julian. We'll drive off without you. Goodbye, Mother! We'll send you a card every single day, we faithfully promise.'

Julian got up on the front of the green caravan. He clicked to Dobby. 'Get on, Dobby! We're off! Goodbye, Mother!'

Dick sat beside him, grinning with pure happiness. The caravans moved off down the drive. George pulled at Trotter's reins and the little horse followed the caravan in front. Anne, sitting beside George, waved wildly.

'Goodbye, Mother! We're off at last on another adventure. Hurrah! Three cheers! Hurrah!'

from **FIVE GO OFF IN A CARAVAN**

SPOOK-TRAINS

'IT'S HEAVENLY walking today,' said Anne. 'Shall we follow a path if we find one or not?'

'Might as well,' said Julian. 'It'll be a bit tiring scrambling through heather all the day.'

So when they did unexpectedly come across a path they followed it. 'It's just a shepherd's path, I expect,' said Dick. 'I bet it's a lonely job, looking after sheep up on these desolate heathery hills.'

They went on for some way, enjoying the stretches of bright heather, the lizards that darted quickly away from their feet and the hosts of butterflies of all kinds that hovered and fluttered. Anne loved the little blue ones best and made up her mind to ask Mr Luffy what all their names were.

They had their lunch on a hilltop overlooking a vast stretch of heather, with grey-white blobs in it here and there – the sheep that wandered everywhere.

And, in the very middle of the meal, Anne heard the same rumbling she had heard before, and then, not far off, out spouted some white smoke from the ground. George went quite pale. Timmy leapt to his feet, growling and barking, his tail down. The boys roared with laughter.

'It's all right, Anne and George. It's only the trains underground here. We knew they ran under the moors and we thought we'd see what you did when you first heard them rumbling, and saw the smoke.'

'I'm not a bit frightened,' said Anne, and the boys looked at her, astonished. It was George who was the scared one! Usually it was quite the other way round.

George got back her colour and laughed. She called Timmy. 'It's all right, Tim. Come here. You know what trains are, don't you?'

The children discussed the trains. It really did seem strange to think of trains in those hollowed-out tunnels down below the moors – the people in them, reading their newspapers and talking – down in tunnels where the sun never shone at all.

'Come on,' said Julian, at last. 'Let's go on. We'll walk to the top of the next slope, and then I think we ought to turn back.'

They found a little path that Julian said must be a rabbit-path, because it was so narrow, and set off, chattering and laughing. They climbed through the heather to the top of the next slope. And at the top they got quite a surprise.

Down in the valley below was a silent and deserted stretch of railway lines! They appeared out of the black hole of a tunnel mouth, ran for about half a mile, and then ended in what seemed to be a kind of railway yard.

'Look at that,' said Julian. 'Old derelict lines – not used any more, I should think. I suppose that tunnel's out of date, too.'

'Let's go down and have a squint,' said Dick. 'Come on! We've got plenty of time, and we can easily go back a shorter way.'

They set off down the hill to the lines. They arrived some way from the tunnel mouth, and followed the lines to the deserted railway yard. There seemed to be nobody about at all.

'Look,' said Dick, 'there are some old wagons on that set of lines over there. They look as if they haven't been used for a hundred years. Let's give them a shove and set them going!'

'Oh, no!' said Anne, afraid. But the two boys and George, who had always longed to play about with real railway trucks, ran over to where three or four stood on the lines. Dick and Julian shoved hard at one. It moved. It ran a little way and crashed into the buffers of another. It made a terrific noise in the silent yard.

from **FIVE GO OFF TO CAMP**

AWAY ON THEIR OWN

They were all ready the next day. Everything was neatly packed and strapped to the bicycles, except for the rucksacks, which each child was to carry on his or her back. The baskets held a variety of food for that day, but when it had been eaten Julian was to buy what they needed.

'I suppose all their brakes are in order?' said Uncle Quentin, thinking he ought to take some interest in the proceedings, and remembering that when he was a boy and had a bicycle, the brakes would never work.

'Oh, Uncle Quentin, of course they're all right,' said Dick. 'We'd never dream of going out on our bikes if the brakes and things weren't in order. The Highway Code is very strict about things like that, you know – and so are we!'

Uncle Quentin looked as if he had never even heard of the Highway Code. It was quite likely he hadn't. He lived in a world of his own, a world of theories and figures and diagrams – and he was eager to get back to it! However, he waited politely for the children to make last-minute adjustments, and then they were ready.

'Goodbye, Aunt Fanny! I'm afraid we shan't be able to write to you, as you won't be able to get in touch with us to let us know where you get fixed up. Never mind, enjoy yourselves,' said Julian.

'Goodbye, Mother! Don't worry about us – we'll be having a jolly good time!' called George.

'Goodbye, Aunt Fanny; goodbye, Uncle Quentin!'

'So long, Uncle! Aunt Fanny, we're off!'

And so they were, cycling down the lane that led away from Kirrin Cottage. Their aunt and uncle stood at the gate, waving till the little party had disappeared round the corner in the sunshine. Timmy was loping along beside George's bicycle, on his long, strong legs, overjoyed at the idea of a really good run.

'Well, we're off,' said Julian, as they rounded the corner. 'What a bit of luck, going off like this by ourselves. Good old Uncle Quentin! I'm glad he made that muddle.'

'Don't let's ride too many miles the first day – I always get so stiff if we do,' said Anne.

'We're not going to,' said Dick. 'Whenever you feel tired just say so – it doesn't matter where we stop!'

from **FIVE GET INTO TROUBLE**

ACROSS THE COUNTRYSIDE

'Yes. We brought everything you told us to,' said Anne. 'Your rucksack looks a bit fuller than ours, Ju!'

'Well, I've got maps and things in it,' said Julian. 'It's a strange place, this moor – miles and miles and miles of it! Strange names on it too – Blind Valley – Rabbit Hill – Lost Lake – Coney Copse!'

'Rabbit Hill! Timmy would love that,' said George, and Timmy pricked up his ears. Rabbits? Ah, that was the kind of place he liked!

'Well, actually we're going towards Rabbit Hill now,' said Julian. 'And after that there's Coney Copse, and as "coney" is a country word for rabbit, Timmy ought to enjoy himself!'

'Woof,' said Timmy joyfully and bounded ahead. He felt very happy. His four friends were with him, their rucksacks were full of delicious-smelling sandwiches, and a long, long walk lay ahead, teeming, he hoped with rabbits!

It was lovely walking along in the sun. They soon left the little village behind and took a winding lane. The hedges on either side became so high that the four couldn't see over the tops at all.

'What a sunken lane!' said Dick. 'I feel as if I'm walking in a tunnel! And how narrow! I wouldn't like to drive a car along this lane. If I met another car I might have to back up for miles!'

'We shan't meet anyone much,' said Julian. 'It's only in the summer that cars come along these lanes – people on holiday, touring round the countryside. Look – we take that path now – it leads to Rabbit Hill, according to the map!'

They climbed over a stile in the high hedge and walked over a field towards a curious little hill. Timmy suddenly went mad with excitement. He could smell rabbits – and he could see them too!

'You don't often see so many rabbits out in the daytime,' said George, surprised.

'Big ones and little ones too – what a scampering.'

They came to the hill and sat down quietly to watch the rabbits. But it was quite impossible to make Timmy do the same. The sight and smell of so many made him quite wild. He pulled away from George's hand and went bounding madly up the hill, scattering rabbits by the dozen.

'Timmy!' yelled George, but for once Timmy paid no attention. He rushed here and rushed there, getting very angry as first one rabbit and then another neatly popped down a hole.

'It's no use calling him,' said Dick. 'He won't catch one, anyway – see how nippy they are. It's my belief they're having a game with our Timmy!'

It did look rather like it. As soon as Timmy had chased two or three rabbits down one hole, a few more would pop up from another behind him. The children laughed. It was as good as a pantomime.

'Where do you mean to have lunch?' asked Anne. 'If we stay here much longer I shall really have to have something to eat – and it's not nearly time yet. I wish I didn't always feel so hungry in the open air.'

'Well, come on then,' said Julian. 'We've got some way to go before we get to our lunch-place. I've made a pretty good timetable of our tour – we're going to go all round the moors and finish at the place we started at! I've really marked it all out pretty well.'

'Do we sleep at farmhouses or something at night?' asked George. 'I should like that. Will they mind having us, do you think? Or do we go to inns?'

'Farmhouses for two nights and inns for the other nights,' said Julian. 'I've marked them all.'

They went up Rabbit Hill and down the other side. There were just as many rabbits there. Timmy chased them till he panted like an engine going uphill!

A PLEASANT MORNING

THE CARAVANS stood on high wheels. There was a window on each side. The door was at the front, and so were the steps, of course. Bright curtains hung at the windows, and a line of bold carving ran round the edges of the out-jutting roof.

'They are old traveller caravans painted and made really up to date,' said Julian. 'They're jolly comfortable inside too – bunks that fold down against the walls in the daytime – a little sink for washing-up, though we usually use the stream, because it's such a bore to fetch water – a small larder, cupboards and shelves – cork carpet on the floor with warm rugs so that no draught comes through . . .'

'You sound as if you are trying to sell them to me!' said George, with a laugh. 'You needn't! I love them both, and I think they're miles nicer than the modern caravans down there. Somehow these seem real!'

'Oh, the others are real enough,' said Julian. 'And they've got more space – but space doesn't matter to us because we shall live outside most of the time.'

'Do we have a campfire?' asked George, eagerly. 'Oh, yes – I see we do. There's the ashy patch where you had your fire. Oh, Julian, do let's have a fire there at night and sit round it in the darkness!'

'With midges biting us and bats flapping all round,' said Dick. 'Yes, certainly we will! Come inside, George.'

'She's to come into my caravan first,' said Anne, and pushed George up the steps. George was really delighted.

She was very happy to think she was going to have a peaceful two weeks here with her three cousins and Timmy. She pulled her bunk up and down to see how it worked. She opened the larder and cupboard doors. Then she went to see the boys' caravan.

'How tidy!' she said, in surprise. 'I expected Anne's to be tidy – but yours is just as spick and span. Oh dear – I hope you haven't all turned over a new leaf and become models of neatness – I haven't!'

'Don't worry,' said Dick, with a grin. 'Anne has been at work – you know how she loves to put everything in its place. We don't need to worry about anything when she's about. Good old Anne!'

'All the same, George will have to help,' said Anne, firmly. 'We've all got to tidy up and cook, and do things like that.'

George groaned. 'All right, Anne, I'll do my share – sometimes. I say – there won't be much room for Timmy on my bunk at nights, will there?'

'Well, he's not coming on mine,' said Anne. 'He can sleep on the floor on a rug. Can't you, Timmy?'

'Woof,' said Timmy, without wagging his tail at all. He looked very disapproving.

'There you are – he says he wouldn't dream of doing such a thing!' said George. 'He always sleeps on my feet.'

They went outside again. It really was a lovely day. The primroses opened more and more of their little yellow flowers, and a blackbird suddenly burst into a fluting song on the bough of a hawthorn tree in the hedge nearby.

'Did anyone get a paper in the village?' asked Dick. 'Oh, you did, Julian. Good. Let's have a look at the weather forecast. If it's good we might go for a long walk this afternoon. The sea is not really very far off.'

Julian took the folded paper from his pocket and threw it over to Dick. He sat down on the steps of the caravan and opened it. He was looking for the paragraph giving the weather.

from **FIVE HAVE A WONDERFUL TIME**

THE HOLIDAY BEGINS

'Blow! I've got a puncture!' said Dick. 'My tyre's going flat. Worst time it could possibly happen!'

Julian glanced down at Dick's back tyre. Then he looked at his watch. 'You've just got time to pump it up and hope for the best,' he said. 'We've got seven minutes before the train goes.'

Dick jumped off and took his pump. The others got off their bicycles, too, and stood round, watching to see if the tyre blew up well or not.

They were on their way to Kirrin Station to catch the train, bicycles and all. Their luggage had gone on in advance, and they thought they had left plenty of time to ride to the station, get their bicycles labelled and put in the luggage van, and catch the train comfortably.

'We can't miss the train!' said George, putting on her best scowl. She always hated it when things went wrong.

'We can. Easiest thing in the world!' said Julian, grinning at George's fierce face. 'What do you say, Timmy?'

Timmy barked sharply, as if to say he certainly agreed. He licked George's hand and she patted him. The scowl left her face as she saw Dick's tyre coming up well. They'd just do it! Dick felt his tyre, gave a sigh of relief, and put his pump back in its place.

'Phew! That was hot work,' he said, mounting his bicycle. 'Hope it will last till we get to the station. I was afraid you'd have to go without me.'

'Oh, no,' said Anne. 'We'd have caught the next train. Come on, Timmy!'

The four cousins and Timmy the dog raced on towards the station. They cycled into the station yard just as the signal went up to show the train was due.

The porter came towards them, his big round face red and smiling.

'I sent your luggage off for you,' he said. 'Not much between you, I must say – just one small trunk!'

'Well, we don't wear much on holidays,' said Julian. 'Can you label our bikes quickly for us? I see the train is due.'

The porter began to label the four bicycles. He didn't hurry. He wouldn't let the train go off again till he had done his job, that was certain. There it was now, coming round the bend.

'You going off to Cornwall, I see?' said the porter. 'And to Tremannon, too. You want to be careful of bathing there. That's a fierce coast and a hungry sea.'

'Oh, do you know it?' said Anne, surprised. 'Is it a nice place?'

'Nice? Well, I dunno about that,' said the porter, raising his voice as the train came rumbling in. 'I used to go out in my uncle's fishing boat all round there, and it's wild and lonely. I shouldn't have thought it was much of a place for a holiday – no pier, no ice cream sellers, no concert parties, no cinema, no . . .'

'Good,' said Julian. 'We can do without all those, thank you. We mean to bathe, and hire a boat, and fish, and bike all round about. That's our kind of holiday!'

'Woof!' said Timmy, wagging his tail.

'Yes, and yours too,' said George, rubbing his big head. 'Come on, we'd better get into a carriage.'

from **FIVE GO DOWN TO THE SEA**

SNIFFER'S PATRINS

Patrins are way-markers left by Travellers, usually made of leaves, grass and twigs.

'Will it be all right if we go up on the moors this afternoon?' asked George.

'Yes, quite all right. But if you want to take your tea, you'll have to pack it yourselves,' said Mrs Johnson. 'I'm taking the small children out for a ride, and there's one on the leading rein still, as you know.'

They were ready to set off at three o'clock, their tea packed and everything. The horses were caught in the field and got ready too. They set off happily.

'Now we'll see if we are as clever as we think we are, at reading traveller patrins!' said George. 'Timmy, don't chase every rabbit you see, or you'll be left behind!'

They cantered up on to the moor, passing the place where the caravans had stood. They knew the direction they had taken, and here and there they saw wheel marks. It was fairly easy to follow their trail, because five caravans made quite a path to follow.

'Here's where they camped first,' said Julian, riding up to a blackened spot that showed where a fire had been lit. 'We ought to find a message left somewhere here.'

They searched for one. George found it. 'It's here, behind this tree!' she called. 'Out of the wind.'

They dismounted and came round George. On the ground was the patrin, the shape of a cross, the long stick pointing forwards in the direction they were going. Other single sticks lay there, to show that a caravan had gone that way, and beside them were the large and the small leaf, weighted with tiny stones.

'What did those leaves show now? Oh yes, Sniffer and his dog!' said Dick. 'Well, we're on the right way, though we'd know that anyhow, by the fire!'

They mounted again and went on. It proved quite easy to find and follow the patrins. Only once did they find any difficulty and that was when they came to a place, marked by two trees, where there was no apparent sign in the heather of any caravan marks.

'The heather's so jolly thick here that it's taken the caravans as if it were a feather bed, springing up when they had gone, and giving no sign of where they had passed,' said Julian. He dismounted and had a good look round. No, there was no sign.

'We'll go on a little way,' he said. 'We may come to a camping place, then we'll know.'

But they came to no old camping place, and stopped at last in bewilderment. 'We've lost the trail,' said Dick. 'We're not such good travellers after all!'

'Let's go back to those two trees,' said George. 'We can still just see them. If it's so easy to lose the way there, there might be a patrin, although there are no camp marks. After all, a patrin is left to show the way, in case the ones following take the wrong route.'

So back they rode to the two trees, and there, sure enough, was Sniffer's patrin! Henry found it set carefully between the trees, so that nothing could disturb it.

'Here's the cross, and the single sticks and the leaves!' she said. 'But look, the long stick of the cross points to the east and we went off to the north. No wonder we found no signs of the caravans!'

They set off to the east this time, across the thick, springy heather, and almost at once found signs of the passing of caravans, twigs broken off the bushes, a wheel rut on a soft piece of ground.

'We're right, now,' said Julian, pleased. 'I was beginning to think it was all too easy for words! But it isn't!'

They rode for two hours, and then decided to have tea. They sat down in a little glade of silver birches, with an unexpected copse of pale primroses behind. Timmy had to make up his mind which to choose, a rabbit chase, or titbits from the children's tea!

OFF TO BILLYCOCK HILL

The sun shone down hotly as the Five sped down the sandy road that ran alongside Kirrin Bay. Timmy loped easily beside them, his tongue hanging out quite a long way. Anne always said that he had the longest tongue of any dog she had ever known!

The sea was as blue as forget-me-nots as they cycled along beside it. Across the bay they could see little Kirrin Island, with Kirrin Castle towering up.

'Doesn't it look fine?' said Dick. 'I half wish we were going to spend Whitsun at Kirrin Cottage, and were going bathing and rowing across to George's little island over there.'

'We can do that in the summer hols,' said Julian. 'It's fun to explore other parts of the country when we can. Toby says the caves in Billycock Hill are marvellous.'

'What's Toby like?' asked George. 'We've never seen him, Anne and I.'

'He's a bit of a joker,' said Dick. 'Likes to put caterpillars down people's necks and so on – and beware if he has a magnificent rose in his buttonhole and asks you to smell it.'

'Why?' asked Anne, surprised.

'Because when you bend down to smell it you'll get a squirt of water in your face,' said Dick. 'It's a trick rose.'

'I don't think I'm going to like him much,' said George, who didn't take kindly to tricks of this sort. 'I'll probably bash him on the head if he does things like that to me.'

'That won't be any good,' said Dick cheerfully. 'He won't bash you back – he'll just think up some worse trick. Don't scowl, George – we're on holiday! Toby's all right – a bit of an ass, that's all.'

They had now left Kirrin Bay behind and were cycling down a country lane, set with hawthorn hedges each side. The may was over now, and the first wild roses were showing pink here and there. A little breeze got up, and was very welcome indeed.

'We'll have an ice when we come to a village,' said Julian after they had cycled about six miles.

'Two ices,' said Anne. 'Oh dear – this hill – what a steep one we've come to. I don't know whether it's worse to ride up slowly and painfully, or to get off and push my bike to the top.'

Timmy tore up to the top in front of them and then sat down to wait in the cool breeze there, his tongue hanging out longer than ever. Julian came to the top first and looked down the other side.

'There's a village there,' he said. 'Right at the bottom. Let's see – yes, it's Tennick village – we'll stop and ask if it sells ices.'

It did, of course – strawberry and vanilla. The four children sat on a seat under a tree outside the small village shop, and dug little wooden spoons into ice-tubs. Timmy sat nearby, watching hopefully. He knew that at least he would be able to lick out the empty tubs.

'Oh, Tim – I didn't mean to buy you one, because you really are a bit fat,' said George, looking at the beseeching brown eyes fixed on her ice cream. 'But as you'll probably get very thin running so far while we're cycling, I'll buy you a whole one for yourself.'

'Wuff,' said Timmy, bounding into the little shop at once and putting his great paws up on the counter, much to the surprise of the woman behind it.

'It's a waste, really, giving Timmy an ice,' said Anne when George and the dog came out. 'He just loosens it with his tongue and gulps it down. I sometimes wonder he doesn't chew up the cardboard tub, too!'

After ten minutes' rest they all set off again, feeling nice and cool inside. It really was lovely cycling through the June countryside – the trees were so fresh and green still, and the fields they passed were golden with buttercups – thousands and thousands of them, nodding their polished heads in the wind.

There was very little traffic on these deserted country roads – an occasional farm cart and sometimes a car, but little else. The Five kept to the lanes as much as they could, for they all preferred their quaint, winding curves set with hedges of all kinds, to the wide, dusty main roads, straight and uninteresting.

'We ought to get to Billycock Farm about four o'clock,' said Dick. 'Or maybe sooner. What time do we have our lunch, Julian? And where?'

'We'll find a good place about one o'clock,' said Julian. 'And not a minute before. So it's no good anyone saying they are hungry yet. It's only twelve.'

'I'm more thirsty than hungry,' said Anne. 'And I'm sure old Timmy must be dying of thirst! Let's stop at the next stream so that he can have a drink.'

'There's one,' said Dick, pointing to where a stream wound across a nearby field. 'Hey, Tim – go and have a drink, old fellow!'

Timmy shot through the hedge to the stream and began to lap. The others dismounted and stood waiting. Anne picked a spray of honeysuckle and put it through a buttonhole of her blouse. 'Now I can sniff it all the time,' she said. 'Delicious!'

'Hey, Tim – leave some water for the fishes!' shouted Dick. 'George, stop him drinking any more. He's swelling up like a balloon.'

'He's not,' said George. 'Timmy! That's enough! Here, boy, here!'

Timmy took one last lap and then raced over to George. He pranced round her, barking joyfully.

'There – he feels much better now,' said George, and away they all went again, groaning as they cycled slowly up the many hills in that part of the country, and shouting with delight as they sped furiously down the other side.

Julian had decided where to have their midday meal – on the top of a high hill! Then they could see all the country for miles around, and there would also be a nice cooling breeze.

'Cheer up,' he said as they came to the steepest hill they had so far encountered. 'We'll have our lunch at the top of this hill – and a good long rest!'

from **FIVE GO TO BILLYCOCK HILL**

MAKING PLANS

It was very exciting making plans to go to the lighthouse. Tinker told them all about it, time and time again.

'It's very tall, and there's an iron stairway – a spiral one – going from the bottom up to the top. And at the top is a little room for the lamp that used to flash to warn ships away.'

'It sounds smashing,' said George. 'What about Timmy, though? Can he climb up a spiral stairway?'

'Well, he can live down at the bottom, can't he, if it's too difficult for him to climb up?' said Tinker. 'Mischief can climb it easily – he simply races up!'

'If Timmy has to live at the bottom, I shall live there with him,' said George.

'Why not wait and see the lighthouse before you arrange the sleeping places?' said Julian, giving her a friendly punch. 'Now first we must find out exactly where it is – and the way to get there. It's a pity Tinker can't turn into a real car – he could run us there in no time!'

Tinker at once imagined himself to be a large van, taking the Five and all their luggage along the road.

He raced round the room, making his usual car noise, and hooting so loudly that he made everyone jump. Julian caught him as he raced round the table and sat him down firmly.

'Any more of that and we leave you behind,' he said. 'Now – where's that map of yours – let's have a look at it – and then we'll get Aunt Fanny's big map of the coast, and track down the road to your lighthouse.'

Soon Tinker and the Five were studying a large-scale map of the coast, Mischief sitting on Dick's shoulder and tickling his neck.

'See – that's the way to go,' said Julian. 'It really wouldn't be far by sea – look, round the coast here, cut across this bay, round the headland – and just there are the rocks on which the old lighthouse stands. But by road it's a very long way.'

'Better go by car, though,' said Dick. 'We've a good bit of luggage to take – not only our clothes, but crockery and things like that. And food.'

'There are still some stores there,' said Tinker, eagerly. 'Dad left some when we went away from the lighthouse.'

'They'll probably have gone bad,' said Julian.

'Well – don't take too much,' said Tinker. 'It's a pretty rough way over the rocks to the lighthouse – there isn't a road that runs right up to it, you know. We shall have to carry everything ourselves, once we get to the place. We can always get fresh food if we want it – the village isn't all that far away – but there are some days when you can't even leave the lighthouse! You see the waves splash house-high over the rocks when there's a rough wind. We'd have to get across by boat if the tide's in – the rocks are covered then!'

'This sounds too exciting for words!' said Dick, his eyes shining. 'What do you think about it, Anne? You haven't said a word!'

'Well – I do feel just a bit scared!' said Anne. 'It sounds so lonely. I do hope no ships will be wrecked on those awful rocks while we're there!'

'Tinker said there was a fine new lighthouse farther along the coast,' said Julian. 'Its light will keep every ship away from that wicked stretch of rocks. Look, Anne, you would like to come, wouldn't you? If not, Aunt Fanny wouldn't mind just you staying here. You're a little mouse – you wouldn't bother Uncle Quentin or the professor at all!'

'I shouldn't dream of not coming with you,' said Anne, indignantly. 'Julian – you don't think there are still wreckers about do you? I should hate that.'

'They belong to years gone by,' said Julian. 'Cheer up, Anne – this is just a little visit we're going to pay to Tinker's seaside house! He is kindly taking in visitors this spring!'

'Well, let's get on with our plans,' said Dick. 'We go there by car – er, what was that you just said, Tinker?'

'I said I'll drive you, if you like,' said Tinker. 'I could dr—'

'You haven't a driving licence, so don't talk nonsense,' said George, crossly.

'I know I haven't – but all the same I can drive!' said Tinker. 'I've driven my father's car round and round our garden, see? And—'

'Oh, do shut up,' said Dick. 'You and your pretend cars! Julian, when shall we go to his lighthouse?'

'Well, why not tomorrow morning?' said Julian. 'I'm sure everyone would be glad if we left as soon as possible! It's hard on Aunt Fanny and Joanna to have so many here. We'll see about a car and someone to drive us, and then we'll pack and make our getaway!'

'Hurray,' said George in delight, and pounded on the table, making Mischief leap up to the top of a bookcase in fright. 'Oh, sorry, Mischief – did I scare you? Timmy tell him I'm sorry, I didn't mean it. He probably understands your doggy language.'

Timmy looked up at Mischief, gave two little whines and a comforting wuff. Mischief listened with his head on one side, and then leapt down, landing neatly on Timmy's back.

'Thanks for giving him my message, Tim,' said George, and everyone laughed. Good old Timmy! He wagged his long tail and put his head on George's knee, looking up at her beseechingly.

'All right, old thing – I understand your language, whether you talk with your voice or your eyes,' said George, patting him. 'You want a walk, don't you?'

'Woof!' said Timmy joyfully, and tore to the door.

from **FIVE GO TO DEMON'S ROCKS**

PLACES THAT INSPIRED THE BOOKS

The Famous Five love to travel and explore, but do the places they visit in the stories exist in real life? Well, you won't find Kirrin village or Kirrin Island on any map of Great Britain, but Enid Blyton did base these and some other places in the books on actual places she had visited or heard about.

KIRRIN CASTLE

In the May 1931 edition of the magazine *Teachers World*, Enid Blyton writes: 'As I drove along in my little car I saw, far away in the distance, a rounded hill, and on it was the ruin of an old, old castle.' A photo printed with the letter shows it to be Corfe Castle in Dorset.

Could this be the castle that gave Enid Blyton the idea for Kirrin Castle? It's certainly very possible. Both castles are built of white stone and have only one large tower still standing. Both have imposing arched entranceways. At Corfe this huge archway has a great break across it, and one side has slipped downwards several metres. In *Five on a Treasure Island* when the Five first go to Kirrin Castle, we are told that they 'gazed at the enormous old archway, now half broken down .

KIRRIN ISLAND

Where did Enid Blyton get the inspiration for Kirrin Island? When was asked if Kirrin was based on a real place, she said: 'Yes. Kirrin was based on an actual village, bay and island but in the Channel Isles, not England.'

We also know that Enid visited Jersey during her honeymoon in 1924, and if we put these two pieces of information together we can see how Enid's imagination took Corfe Castle in Dorset, placed it on an island she had visited in the Channel Islands many years before, and gave us Kirrin Island, complete with ruined castle, rabbits and jackdaws.

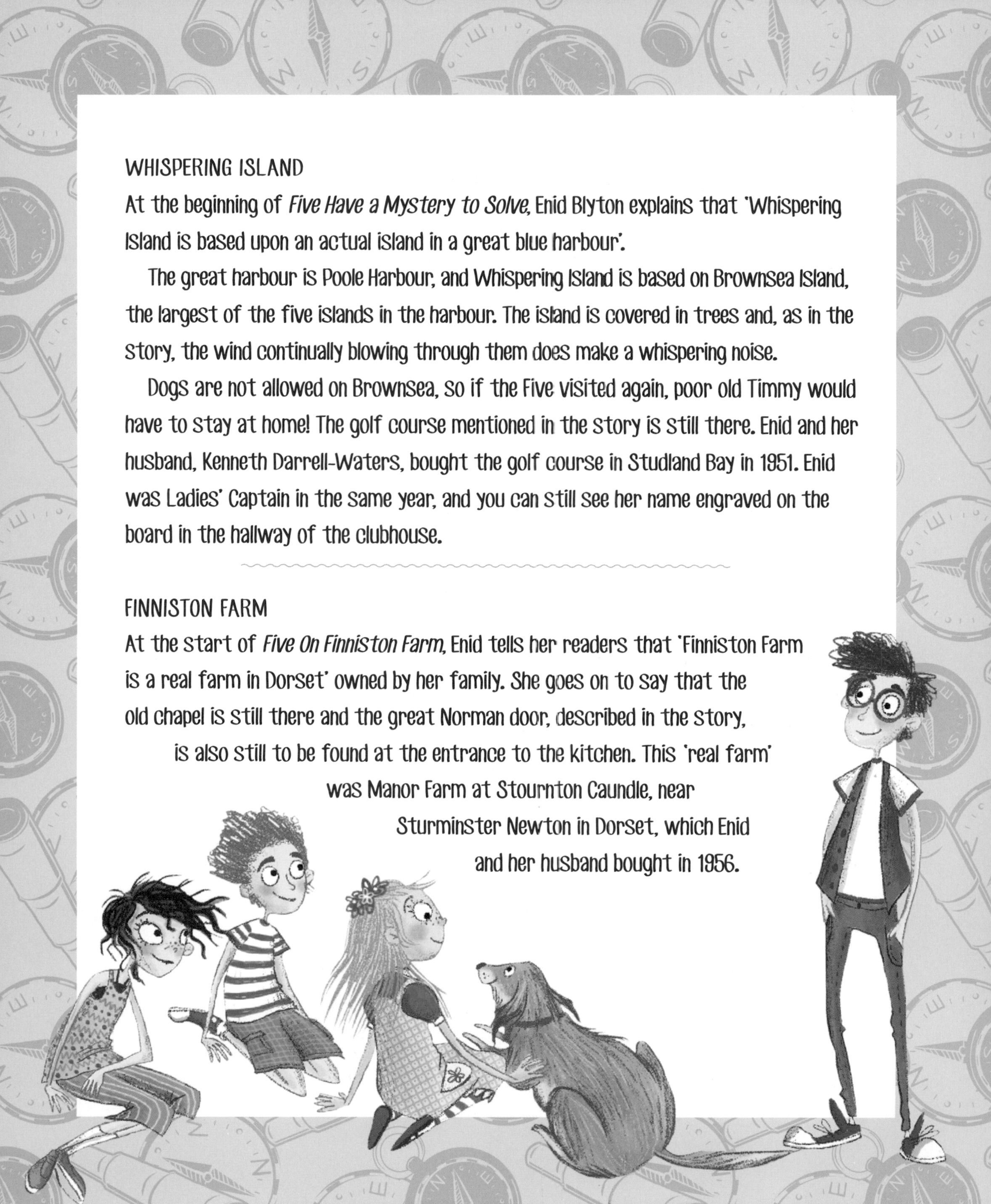

WHISPERING ISLAND

At the beginning of *Five Have a Mystery to Solve*, Enid Blyton explains that 'Whispering Island is based upon an actual island in a great blue harbour'.

The great harbour is Poole Harbour, and Whispering Island is based on Brownsea Island, the largest of the five islands in the harbour. The island is covered in trees and, as in the story, the wind continually blowing through them does make a whispering noise.

Dogs are not allowed on Brownsea, so if the Five visited again, poor old Timmy would have to stay at home! The golf course mentioned in the story is still there. Enid and her husband, Kenneth Darrell-Waters, bought the golf course in Studland Bay in 1951. Enid was Ladies' Captain in the same year, and you can still see her name engraved on the board in the hallway of the clubhouse.

FINNISTON FARM

At the start of *Five On Finniston Farm*, Enid tells her readers that 'Finniston Farm is a real farm in Dorset' owned by her family. She goes on to say that the old chapel is still there and the great Norman door, described in the story, is also still to be found at the entrance to the kitchen. This 'real farm' was Manor Farm at Stournton Caundle, near Sturminster Newton in Dorset, which Enid and her husband bought in 1956.

GET TO KNOW ANNE

Anne is the younger sister of Julian and Dick. She likes wearing dresses and playing with dolls (but in other ways is not so dissimilar to her cousin George). Just like George, Anne prides herself on her honesty. She likes horse riding and becomes captain of games in her class at her school. She is sensible, brave when she needs to be, and clever.

It has to be said, though, that Anne isn't a fan of adventures. She dislikes being in enclosed spaces and encountering creepy-crawlies.

Anne is brilliant at organising her siblings and cousin, and sorting out meals and other arrangements wherever she happens to be. Although she is quiet, she won't always let others get the better of her – Julian once described her as changing from a mouse into a tiger.

Anne says

You know, most of our hols have been packed with adventures - awfully exciting, I know - but I'd like an ordinary holiday now, wouldn't you - not too exciting?

Other people say

Anne has been at work – you know how she loves to put everything in its place. We don't need to worry about anything when she's about. Good old Anne!

SUMMER with THE FAMOUS FIVE

A LAZY AFTERNOON

'It's hot!' said Julian, fanning himself with a paper. 'What are we all going to do this afternoon?'

'Nothing!' said Dick at once. 'I feel as if I'm rapidly melting. It's even too hot to go swimming.'

'Let's have a lazy afternoon for once,' said George. 'If anyone suggests a walk or a bike ride in this heat, I'll scream.'

'Woof,' said Timmy at once.

'He's suggesting a walk, George,' said Anne, with a laugh. 'Scream!'

'Too hot even for that,' said George. 'Let's find a cool, shady place, take our books, and either read or snooze till tea-time. I'd enjoy a lazy afternoon for once.'

'Woof,' said Timmy mournfully, not agreeing at all.

'Come on, then,' said Julian. 'We'll go to that little copse we know, under those leafy trees – near that tiny stream that ripples along and makes a nice cool noise!'

'Well – I think I can just about walk there,' said Dick, and they all set off, strolling along, unable to keep up with the lively, energetic Timmy.

'It makes me hot even to look at Timmy,' complained Dick. 'Hot to hear him too, puffing like a steam train. Put your tongue in, Timmy, I can't bear to look at it.'

Timmy ran ahead, glad that they were off for what appeared to be a walk. He was very disappointed when the others flopped down in a little copse under some big leafy trees near a small brook. He stood looking at them in disgust.

'Sorry, Tim. No walkies,' said George. 'Come and sit down with us. For goodness sake, don't go rabbiting in this weather.'

'It'd be a waste of your time, Timmy,' said Dick. 'All sensible bunnies are having an afternoon snooze, down at the bottom of their holes, waiting for the cool evening to come.'

'Woof,' said Timmy in scorn, watching the four arrange themselves comfortably under a canopy made by young saplings and bushes.

Branches from big trees nearby overhung them, and by the time the four had wriggled themselves well into the little thicket, not a single sunbeam could reach them. In fact, it was difficult to see them, so well hidden were they in the green shade.

'This is better,' said George. 'I think it's about the coolest spot we'll find anywhere. Doesn't that little stream sound nice, too, gurgling away over the stones? I think I'm going to sleep – and if you dare to flop yourself down on my middle, Timmy, I'll send you home!'

Timmy stood and looked at the well-hidden four. His tail drooped. What was the point of coming to a wood, to lie down and do nothing? Well – he was going rabbiting! He swung round, pushed his way out of the thicket, and disappeared.

George raised her head to look after him.

'He's gone rabbiting after all,' she said. 'Well, I hope he remembers where we are and comes back at tea-time. Now for a lazy – peaceful – quiet afternoon!'

'Don't talk so much,' said Dick, and got a sideways kick from George's foot.

'Oh, I feel sleepy!'

In a few minutes' time not one of the four was awake.

Books lay unopened on the ground.

A small beetle ran over Anne's bare leg, and she didn't even feel it.

A robin hopped on to a branch just above Dick's face, but his eyes were closed and he didn't see it.

It certainly was a hot afternoon. Nobody was about at all. Not a sound was to be heard except for the running water nearby, and a yellowhammer somewhere who persisted in saying that he wanted 'a little bit of bread and no cheese'. The four were as sound asleep as if they were in bed.

And then, far away on a road that bordered the wood, a motorbike came by. It had a sidecar, and it made quite a noise. But the four sleepers heard nothing.

They didn't know that the motorbike had slowed down and turned into the wood, taking one of the grassy woodland walks that wound here and there, quiet and cool.

The motorbike came slowly down one of the paths, not making very much noise now, because it was going slowly. It came near to the little copse where the children lay hidden in the cool shade of the bushes.

The engine of the motorbike gave a sudden little cough as it came along, and Julian awoke with a start.

What was that noise? He listened, but he could hear nothing more because the motorbike, with its sidecar, had now stopped.

Julian shut his eyes again. But he opened them immediately because he heard voices – low voices. People must be somewhere near. Where were they? Julian hoped they wouldn't disturb the four in their cool hiding place. He made a little peephole in the bush he was lying under, and spied through it.

Julian saw the motorbike and sidecar on the grassy path some way off. He saw two men, one just getting out of the sidecar. Julian didn't like the look of them at all.

'What nasty-looking men!' he thought. 'What are they doing here in the middle of a summer's afternoon?'

At first the men talked in low voices, and then an argument started. One raised his voice. 'I tell you, we were followed! It's the only thing to do, to come here and dump the stuff!'

A small bag was dragged out of the sidecar. The second man seemed to be grumbling, not at all willing to do what the other wanted.

'I tell you, I know it won't be found if we put it there,' said the first man. 'What's the matter with you? We can't afford to be stopped with the stuff on us –

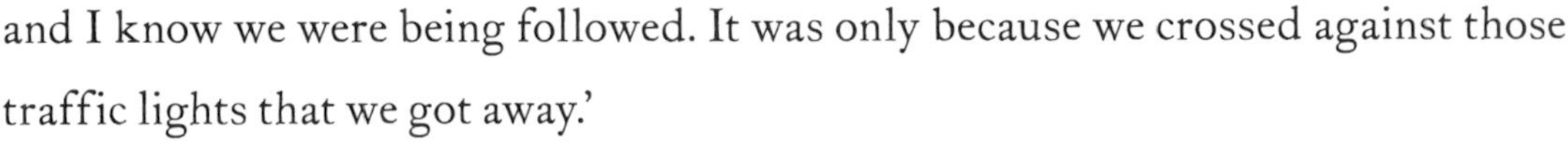

and I know we were being followed. It was only because we crossed against those traffic lights that we got away.'

Julian awoke the others, and whispered to them. Something strange was happening!

Soon all the four were peeping through leafy peepholes at what was going on.

They saw what looked like a small mailbag on the ground by the motorbike.

'What are they going to do with it?' whispered George. 'Should we burst out on them?'

'I would if we had Timmy with us,' whispered back Julian. 'But he's gone rabbiting and may be miles away.'

'And these crooks would be more than a match for us,' said Dick. 'We daren't even show ourselves. We can only watch.'

'I hope we see where they hide the stuff, whatever it is,' said Anne, trying to spy through the leaves. 'There they go with the bag.'

'I can see them,' said Dick, almost forgetting to whisper in his excitement. 'They're climbing a tree!'

'Yes – one's already up, and the other's passing the bag to him,' whispered Julian. 'It must have a hollow trunk, I think. Oh, I wish Timmy was here!'

'Now the second man's trying to climb up, too,' said George. 'The first one wants help, I suppose. The bag must be stuck.'

Both men were now up the tree, trying to stuff the bag down some kind of hollow there. At last there was a thud as if the bag had dropped down.

'If only Timmy was here!' said Julian again. 'It's maddening to lie here and do nothing – but we'd be no match for those two men!'

Then a sudden noise came to their ears – the scampering of feet. Then came a familiar sound. 'Woof!'

'Timmy!' yelled Julian and George together, and Julian leapt up and pushed his way out of his hiding place at once. 'Tell Tim to guard that tree, George, quick!'

'Here, Timmy – on guard!' shouted George, and the astonished Timmy ran to the tree where the two men were staring down in sudden horror.

Timmy gave a blood-curdling growl and one man, who had been about to jump down, shrank back.

'Call that dog off!' he yelled. 'What do you think you're doing?'

'You tell us what you're doing,' said Julian. 'What's in the bag you pushed down that tree hollow?'

'What bag? What are you talking about? You must be mad!' said the man. 'Call that dog off, or I'll report you to the police.'

'Right! We'll report you at the same time!' said Julian. 'You'll stay up that tree till we bring the police back here – and I warn you, if you try jumping down and running away, you'll be sorry. You've no idea what sharp teeth that dog has!'

The two men were so angry that they could hardly speak. Timmy barked loudly, and kept leaping up to try to reach them.

Julian turned to the others. 'Go to the main road and stop a car. Go to the nearest police station and tell the police there to send men here at once. Hurry up.'

But before the others could go off, there came the sound of another motorbike – and then a second – bumping along the woodland path. Julian fell silent. Were more crooks coming? Timmy would be a great help, if so. Julian and the others got behind trees and watched to see who was on the coming motorbikes.

'The police!' yelled Dick, suddenly seeing the familiar uniform. 'They must have been the ones chasing those men. Somebody must have given them the tip that they had turned off into the wood! Hey! We can help you!'

The two policemen stopped in surprise. They saw the motorbike and sidecar.

'Have you kids seen anything of two men with a bag?' shouted one of them.

'Yes. The bag's stuffed down a tree over there, and our dog's guarding the men – they're up in the tree!' shouted back Julian, going towards the police. 'You've just come in time to collect them!'

'Good stuff!' said the policeman with a grin, as he saw the two scared men up the tree, with Timmy still leaping up hopefully at them. 'The bag's up there, too, is it?'

'Down in the hollow of the tree,' said Julian.

'Well, thanks very much for doing our job for us,' said the second policeman. 'We've got some pals on the main road,' he said. 'We said we'd shout if we found anything. They'll soon be along.' He looked at the two men in the tree. 'Well, Jim and Stan? You thought you'd fooled us, didn't you? Are you coming quietly – or do we ask the dog to help us round you up?'

Jim and Stan took one look at the eager Timmy. 'We'll come quietly,' they said, and, when three more men came racing down the woodland path, there was no trouble at all.

Jim and Stan went off with the policemen, Timmy gave one last fierce bark, and all Five watched the men, the motorbikes, and the sidecar disappear with many bumps up the path back to the main road.

'Well!' said George. 'Talk about a nice cool, lazy afternoon! I'm hotter than ever now!'

'Woof,' said Timmy, his tongue hanging out almost to the ground. He looked very hot, too.

'Well, you shouldn't go rabbiting,' said George. 'No wonder you're hot!'

'It's a very good thing he did go rabbiting!' said Dick. 'If he'd been with us, he'd have barked, and those men would have known we were here – and would have gone further on to hide their goods. We'd never have seen what they were doing, or have been able to catch them.'

'Yes. That's true,' said George, and patted Timmy. 'All right, Timmy – you were right to go rabbiting and to come back when you did!'

'Tea-time, everybody!' said Dick, looking at his watch. 'Well – what a very nice, peaceful, lazy afternoon! I really have enjoyed it!'

ICE CREAM FOR TIMMY

'There's the ice cream man,' said Julian, sitting up and feeling for the waterproof pocket in the belt of his bathing trunks. 'Let's have one each.'

'Woof,' said Timmy, and thumped his tail on the sand.

'Yes, all right – one for you, too,' said Dick. 'Though what sense there is in giving you one, I don't know. One lick, one swallow, and it's gone. It might be a fly for all you taste of it.'

Timmy gulped his ice cream down at once and then went into George's hole, squeezing beside her, hoping for a lick of her ice, too. But she pushed him away.

'No, Timmy. Ice cream's wasted on you! You can't even have a lick of mine. And do get back into your hole – you're making me frightfully hot.'

Timmy obligingly got out and went into Anne's hole. She gave him a little bit of her ice cream. He sat panting beside her, looking longingly at the rest of the ice. 'You're melting it with your hot breath,' said Anne. 'Go into Julian's hole now!'

The five of them had a thoroughly lazy morning. As none of them had a watch, they went in far too early for lunch, and were shooed out again by Joanna.

'How you can come in at ten past twelve for a one o'clock lunch, I don't know!' she scolded. 'I haven't even finished the housework yet.'

'Well – it felt like one o'clock,' said Anne, disappointed to find there was so long to wait. Still, when lunch-time came, Joanna really did them well.

'Cold ham and tongue – cold baked beans – beetroot – crisp lettuce straight from the garden – heaps of tomatoes – cucumber – hard-boiled egg!' recited Anne in glee.

'Just the kind of meal I like,' said Dick, sitting down. 'What's for pudding?'

'There it is on the sideboard,' said Anne. 'Wobbly blancmange, fresh fruit salad and jelly. I'm glad I'm hungry.'

'Now, don't you give Timmy any of that ham and tongue,' Joanna warned

George. 'I've got a fine bone for him. Coming, Timmy?'

Timmy knew the word 'bone' very well indeed. He trotted after Joanna at once.

from **FIVE FALL INTO ADVENTURE**

DOWN IN THE COVE

'Let's go down to the sea and bathe,' said Dick. 'We'll go on our bikes and Yan won't be able to pop up and watch us there.'

They took their bicycles and rode off to the coast. Mrs Penruthlan made them sandwiches and gave them fruit cake and drinks to take with them. They saw Yan watching them from behind a hedge as they went.

They took the road to the sea. It was no more than a narrow lane, and wound about like a stream, twisting and turning so that they couldn't get up any speed at all.

'Look – the sea!' cried Dick as they rounded one last bend. The lane had run down between two high, rocky cliffs, and in front of them was a cove into which raced enormous breakers, throwing spray high into the air.

They left their bicycles at the top of the cove, and went behind some big rocks to change into bathing things. When they came out, Julian looked at the sea. It was calm beyond the rocks, but over these the waters raged fiercely and it was impossible to venture in.

They walked a little way round the cliffs, and came to a great pool lying in a rock hollow. 'Just the thing!' cried George and plunged in. 'Gosh, it's cold!'

It should have been hot from the sun, but every now and again an extra large wave broke right into the pool itself, bringing in cooler water. It was fun when that happened. The four of them swam to their hearts' content, and Timmy had a fine time too.

They picnicked on the rocks, with spray flying round them, and then went to explore round the foot of the cliffs.

'This is exciting,' said George. 'Caves, and more caves, and yet more caves! And cove after cove, all as lovely as the one before. I suppose when the tide's in, all these coves are shoulder-high in water.'

'My word, yes,' said Julian, who was keeping a very sharp eye indeed on the tide. 'And a good many of these caves would be flooded too. No wonder Mrs Penruthlan warned us so solemnly about the tides here! I wouldn't want to try and climb up these cliffs if we were caught!'

Anne looked up and shivered. They were so very steep and high. They frowned down at her as if to say, 'We stand no nonsense from anyone! So look after yourself!'

from **FIVE GO DOWN TO THE SEA**

AT KIRRIN COTTAGE

'I feel as if we've been at Kirrin for about a month already!' said Anne, stretching herself out on the warm sand, and digging her toes in. 'And we've only just come!'

'Yes – it's funny how we settle down at Kirrin so quickly,' said Dick. 'We only came yesterday, and I agree with you, Anne – it seems as if we've been here ages. I love Kirrin.'

'I hope this weather lasts out the three weeks we've got left of the holiday,' said Julian, rolling away from Timmy, who was pawing at him, trying to make him play. 'Go away, Timmy. You're too energetic. We've bathed, had a run, played ball – and that's quite enough for a little while. Go and play with the crabs!'

'Woof!' said Timmy, disgusted. Then he pricked up his ears as he heard a tinkling noise from the promenade. He barked again.

'Trust old Timmy to hear the ice cream man,' said Dick. 'Anyone want an ice cream?'

Everyone did, so Anne collected the money and went off to get the ice creams, Timmy close at her heels. She came back with five cartons of ice cream, Timmy jumping up at her all the way.

'I can't think of anything nicer than lying down on hot sand with the sun on every part of my body, eating an ice cream, and knowing there are still three weeks' holiday in front of us – at Kirrin too!' said Dick.

'Yes. It's heaven,' said Anne. 'It's a pity your father has visitors today, George. Who are they? Have we got to dress up for them?'

'I don't think so,' said George. 'Timmy, you've eaten your ice cream in one gulp. What a frightful waste!'

'When are these people coming?' asked Dick.

'About half past twelve,' said George. 'They're coming to lunch – but thank goodness Father told Mother he didn't want a pack of children gobbling all round him and his friends at lunch, so Mother said we could go in at half past twelve, say how-do-you-do and then clear off again with a picnic basket.'

'I must say I think your father has some good ideas at times,' said Dick. 'I suppose they are some scientist friends of his?'

'Yes. Father's working on some great scheme with these two men,' said George. 'One of them's a genius, apparently, and has hit on an idea that's too wonderful for words.'

* * *

'Does anyone feel like another bathe?'

'No. But I don't mind going and lying in the very edge of the sea, and letting the waves there just curl over me,' said Dick. 'I'm absolutely baked lying here.'

'It sounds lovely,' said Anne. 'But the hotter you are the colder the water feels.'

'Come on!' said Dick, getting up. 'I shall hang my tongue out and pant like Timmy soon.'

They all went down to the edge of the water and lay down flat in the tiny curling waves there. Anne gave a little shriek.

'It feels icy! I knew it would. I can't lie down in it yet – I can only sit up!'

However they were soon all lying full-length in the shallow waves at the edge of the sea, sliding down the sand a little every now and again as the tide ebbed farther from them. It was lovely to feel the cool fingers of the sea on every part of them.

Suddenly Timmy barked. He was not in the water with them, but was just at the edge. He thought that lying down in the sea was quite unnecessary! George raised her head.

'What's the matter?' she said. 'There's nobody coming.'

But Dick had heard something too. He sat up hurriedly. 'Gosh, I believe that's someone ringing a bell for us. It sounds like the bell from Kirrin Cottage!'

'But it can't be dinner-time yet!' said Anne in dismay.

'It must be,' said Julian, leaping up. 'Blow! This is what comes of leaving my watch in my anorak pocket! I ought to have remembered that time at Kirrin goes more quickly than anywhere else!'

from **FIVE HAVE PLENTY OF FUN**

THE FIVE ARE ALL TOGETHER AGAIN

'Phew!' said Julian, mopping his wet forehead. 'What a day! Let's go and live at the equator – it would be cool compared to this!'

He stood leaning on his bicycle, out of breath with a long steep ride up a hill. Dick grinned at him. 'You're out of training, Ju!' he said. 'Let's sit down for a bit and look at the view. We're pretty high up!'

They leant their bicycles against a nearby gate and sat down, their backs against the lower bars. Below them spread the Dorset countryside, shimmering in the heat of the day, the distance almost lost in a blue haze. A small breeze came wandering round, and Julian sighed in relief.

'I'd never have come on this biking trip if I'd guessed it was going to be as hot as this!' he said.

'Good thing Anne didn't come – she'd have given up the first day.'

'George wouldn't have minded,' said Dick. 'She's game enough for anything.'

'Good old Georgina,' said Julian, shutting his eyes. 'I'll be glad to see the girls again. Fun to be on our own of course – but things always seem to happen when the four of us are together.'

'Five, you mean,' said Dick, tipping his cap over his eyes. 'Don't forget old Timmy. What a dog! Never knew one that had such a wet lick as Tim. I say – won't it be fun to meet them all! Don't let's forget the time, Julian. Hey, wake up, stupid! If we go to sleep now we won't be in time to meet the girls' bus.'

Julian was almost asleep. Dick looked at him and laughed. Then he looked at his watch, and did a little calculating. It was half past two.

'Let's see now – Anne and George will be on the bus that stops at Finniston Church at five past three,' he thought. 'Finniston is about a mile away, down this hill. I'll give old Julian fifteen minutes to have a nap – and hope to goodness I

don't fall asleep myself!'

He felt his own eyes closing after a minute, and got up at once to walk about. The two girls and Tim must be met, because they would have suitcases with them, which the boys planned to wheel along on their bicycles.

The Five were going to stay at a place called Finniston Farm, set on a hill above the little village of Finniston. None of them had been there before, nor even heard of it. It had all come about because George's mother had heard from an old school friend, who had told her that she was taking paying guests at her farmhouse – and had asked her to recommend visitors to her. George had promptly said she would like to go there with her cousins in the summer holidays.

'Hope it's a good place!' thought Dick, gazing down into the valley, where cornfields waved in the little breeze. 'Anyway, we shall only be there for two weeks – and it will be fun to be together again.'

He looked at his watch. 'Time to go!' He gave Julian a push. 'Hey – wake up!'

''Nother ten minutes,' muttered Julian, trying to turn over, as if he were in bed. He rolled against the gate-bars and fell on to the hard dry earth below. He sat up in surprise. 'Gosh – I thought I was in bed!' he said. 'I could have gone on sleeping for hours.'

'Well, it's time to go and meet that bus,' said Dick. 'I've had to walk about all the time you were asleep, I was so afraid I'd go off myself. Come on, Julian – we really must go!'

They rode down the hill, going cautiously round the sharp corners, remembering how many times they had met herds of cows, wide farm carts, tractors and the like, on their way through this great farming county.

Ah – there was the village, at the bottom of the hill.

It looked old and peaceful and half-asleep.

'Thank goodness it sells ginger beer and ice creams!' said Dick, seeing a small shop with a big sign in the window. 'I feel as if I want to hang out my tongue, like

Timmy does, I'm so thirsty!'

'Let's find the church and the bus stop,' said Julian. 'I saw a spire as we rode down the hill, but it disappeared when we got near the bottom.'

'There's the bus!' said Dick, as he heard the noise of wheels rumbling along in the distance. 'Look, here it comes. We'll follow it.'

'There's Anne in it – and George, look!' shouted Julian. 'We're here exactly on time! Hey, George!'

The bus came to a stop by the old church, and out jumped Anne and George, each with a suitcase – and out leapt old Timmy too, his tongue hanging down, very glad to be out of the hot, jerky, smelly bus.

'There are the boys!' shouted George, and waved wildly as the bus went off again. 'Julian! Dick! I'm so glad you're here to meet us!'

The two boys rode up, and jumped off their bikes, while Timmy leapt round them, barking madly. They thumped the girls on their backs, and grinned at them. 'Just the same old couple!' said Dick. 'You've got a spot on your chin, George, and why on earth have you tied your hair into a ponytail, Anne?'

'You're not very polite, Dick,' said George, bumping him with her suitcase. 'I can't think why Anne and I looked forward so much to seeing you again. Here, take my suitcase – haven't you any manners?'

'Plenty,' said Dick, and grabbed the case. 'I just can't get over Anne's new hair-do. I don't like it, Anne – do you, Ju? Ponytail! A donkey tail would suit you better Anne!'

'It's all right – it's just because the back of my neck was so hot,' said Anne, shaking her hair free in a hurry. She hated her brothers to find fault with her. Julian gave her arm a squeeze.

'Nice to see you both,' he said. 'What about some ginger beer and ice cream? There's a shop over there that sells them. And I've a sudden longing for nice juicy plums!'

'You haven't said a word to Timmy yet,' said George, half offended. 'He's been trotting round you and licking your hands – and he's so dreadfully hot and thirsty!'

'Shake paws, Tim,' said Dick, and Timmy politely put up his right paw. He shook hands with Julian too and then promptly went mad, careering about and almost knocking over a small boy on a bicycle.

'Come on, Tim – want an ice cream?' said Dick, laying his hand on the big dog's head. 'Hark at him panting, George – I bet he wishes he could unzip his hairy coat and take it off! Don't you Tim?'

'Woof!' said Tim, and slapped his tail against Dick's legs.

They all trooped into the ice cream shop. It was half dairy, half baker's. A small girl of about ten came to serve them.

'Mum's lying down,' she said. 'What can I get you? Ice creams, I suppose? That's what everyone wants today.'

'You supposed right,' said Julian. 'A large one each, please – five in all – and four bottles of ginger pop as well.'

'Five ice creams – do you want one for that dog, then?' said the girl in surprise, looking at Timmy.

'Woof,' he said at once.

'There you are,' said Dick, 'he said yes!'

Soon the Five were eating their cold ice creams, Timmy licking his from a saucer. Before he had had many licks, the ice cream slid from the saucer, and Timmy chased it all the way round the shop, as it slid away from his vigorous licks. The little girl watched him, fascinated.

from **FIVE ON FINNISTON FARM**

FUN ON THE BEACH!

If you're lucky enough to visit a beach this summer, as the Famous Five do in the story called *Good Old Timmy* and many of their other adventures, what will you get up to? There's lots to do even when you're not swimming – or scoffing ice creams. How about playing some of these brilliant games?

BEACH LIMBO

Two people hold a skipping rope (or swimming noodle or even a long stick) for others to limbo dance underneath. As each round is complete, lower the height a little bit more.

DEEPEST DIGGER

Who can dig the deepest hole in ten minutes? If Timmy's there, he's bound to be the winner!

BUCKET RELAY

Give everyone a bucket and something that will carry water, e.g. an empty yoghurt pot, a plastic cup or even a big shell. Of course, everyone must have one of an equal size. Each person has to run to the water's edge to fill their container, then run back to put the water in the bucket. First one to fill their bucket wins!

BEACH ART

Collect pebbles, seaweed, sticks, shells and other natural objects found on the beach to create unique pictures on the sand.

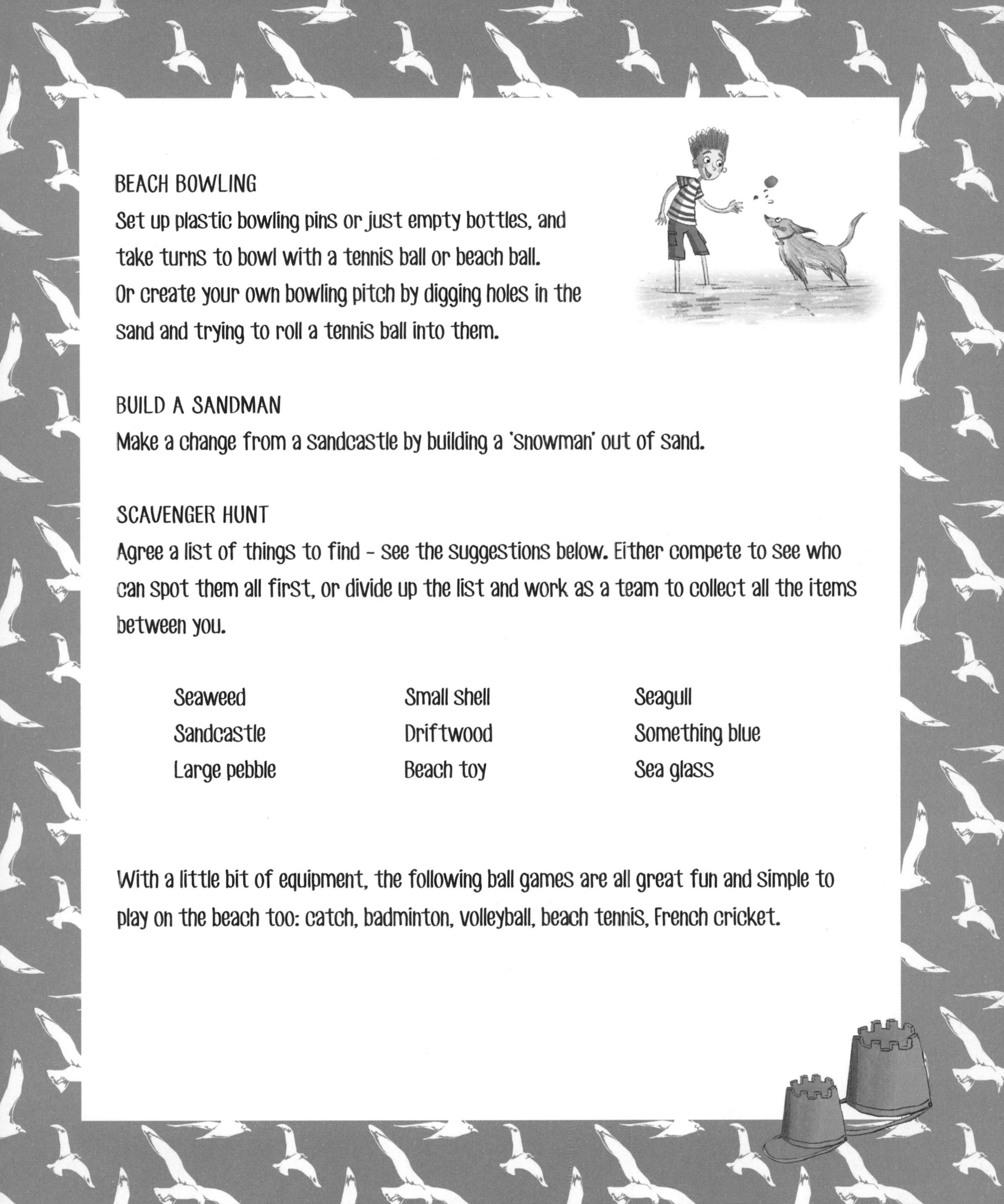

BEACH BOWLING

Set up plastic bowling pins or just empty bottles, and take turns to bowl with a tennis ball or beach ball. Or create your own bowling pitch by digging holes in the sand and trying to roll a tennis ball into them.

BUILD A SANDMAN

Make a change from a sandcastle by building a 'snowman' out of sand.

SCAVENGER HUNT

Agree a list of things to find – see the suggestions below. Either compete to see who can spot them all first, or divide up the list and work as a team to collect all the items between you.

Seaweed	Small shell	Seagull
Sandcastle	Driftwood	Something blue
Large pebble	Beach toy	Sea glass

With a little bit of equipment, the following ball games are all great fun and simple to play on the beach too: catch, badminton, volleyball, beach tennis, French cricket.

GET TO KNOW TIMMY

Timothy is a big, brown mongrel dog. He is George's soulmate – they've been inseparable since she found him as a puppy on the moor. But for quite some time, she had to keep him a secret from her parents.

Timmy can be boisterous when he is being friendly, but he can also be fierce and alarming when he's angered. He can even frighten other dogs – although he is fond of many animals like Trotter, the milkman's horse. Criminals think he is an easy target but they underestimate his cleverness and his loyalty to the rest of the Five. He loves to roam free and hates being locked up on car journeys or train rides, although he enjoys riding out to sea in boats.

Other people say

As a dog, Timothy was far from perfect. He was the wrong shape, his head was too big, his ears were too pricked, his tail was too long. But he was such a mad, friendly, clumsy, laughable creature that every one of the children adored him at once.

He never minds how far we run.

Timmy says

WOOF!

Enid Blyton®

is one of the most popular children's authors of all time.
Her books have sold over 500 million copies and have been translated into other languages more often than any other children's author.

Enid Blyton adored writing for children. She wrote over 600 books and hundreds of short stories. *The Famous Five* books, now 75 years old, are her most popular. She is also the author of other favourites including *The Secret Seven*, *The Magic Faraway Tree*, *Malory Towers* and *Noddy*.

Born in London in 1897, Enid lived much of her life in Buckinghamshire and adored dogs, gardening and the countryside. She was very knowledgeable about trees, flowers, birds and animals. Dorset – where some of the Famous Five's adventures are set – was a favourite place of hers too.

Enid Blyton's stories are read and loved by millions of children (and grown-ups) all over the world.

Visit enidblyton.co.uk to discover more.

THE
FAMOUS
FIVE